EX LIBRIS

THE BAFFLE BOOK

THE
BAFFLE
BOOK

Fifteen Fiendishly Challenging
Detective Puzzles

by

LASSITER WREN & RANDLE MCKAY

originators of the detective problem form

illustrated with diagrams and charts

DAVID R. GODINE · *Publisher*
Boston

This edition published in 2006 *by*
DAVID R. GODINE · *Publisher*
Post Office Box 450
Jaffrey, New Hampshire 03452
www.godine.com

Adapted from *The Baffle Book*, originally published in 1928
for the Crime Club, Inc., by Doubleday, Doran & Company, Inc.

LIBRARY OF CONGRESS
CATALOGING-IN-PUBLICATION DATA
Wren, Lassiter.
The baffle book : fifteen fiendishly challenging detective puzzles /
by Lassiter Wren & Randle McKay.
p.   cm.
Originally published: Garden City, N.Y. :
Doubleday, Doran, 1928–30.
ISBN 1-56792-319-4 (softcover : alk. paper)
1. Detective and mystery stories.   2. Puzzles.
I. McKay, Randle.
II. Title.
GV1511.D4W7   2006
793.73—dc22
2006022123

Fourth Printing, 2017
Printed in the United States of America

WHAT IS YOUR SCORE FOR THE BAFFLE BOOK?

Score your credits here. A total of 75 is good. 100, excellent. 125, remarkable. 150 (maximum), amazing!

Carry forward ......

Answers to the questions printed at the end of each problem will be found in the Answer Section, printed upside-down in the back of the book.

The highest possible score is 150 – that is, 10 credits each for the 15 mysteries or detective problems.

THE BAFFLE BOOK

FOR ALL WHO REVEL IN CRIME DETECTION

HOW OFTEN HAVE YOU been week-ending at the Duchess's place only to have the butler break in on the festive company with the tragic announcement that the master has been found slain in the billiard room, an Oriental dagger driven through his breast? And, fastened to the hilt by ribbon obviously from a wedding-cake box, a note – heliotrope-scented – on which is scrawled: "At last!" But the murderer has not signed it, and no one recognizes the handwriting. And there you are – everyone flabbergasted and in utter confusion. No one, not even the Homicide Squad, can make anything out of the clues, so the whole company, including yourself, is suspected of the crime.

A nice pickle to be in! And why? Simply because you never developed your latent powers of observation and deduction – those qualities of mind which make the solution of the most inscrutable mysteries a veritable pleasure. Confess it, you never heeded Conan Doyle; you thought it was all tosh. But it isn't, as this book will show.

A NEW AND CHALLENGING SPORT

The Baffle Book, with its mysteries and detective problems to be solved from given data and clues, will soon convert you to the enormous importance of observation and deduction. Solve a few dozen of the hypothetical crime mysteries that follow and you will be equipped to work out any given crime at any given house-party at any given moment.

"What do you deduce?" will be the question on everyone's lips as soon as the *Baffle Book* reaches the public. Here are the evidences of the crime. These are the facts established by the police. What do you observe? Which are the telltale clues? What do you deduce? How will you answer the questions asked of you at the end of each mystery problem: "Who is guilty?" or "What motive?" etc. As you use your reasoning powers in the solution of each problem, so you will be rated according to the credits specified in the book. And if you are really baffled, then you can look up the true solution in the Answer Section in the back of the book. (To consult this, shut the book, turn it upside down and open the book again as usual. The answers are printed upside-down to deter you from looking too quickly for the solutions of the mysteries. It is more fun to work them out for yourself first.)

★　★　★

YOU WILL BE BAFFLED

Most of the mysteries are not easy to solve at first glance. That is what makes them interesting. But each has a logical and absolute solution which can be deduced reasonably by any intelligent and well-informed person. You must consider all the circumstances of the crime or mystery as stated in the text or as given in the chart or diagram or illustration, if one accompanies the problem. Any, or all together, may yield the clue or clues essential for the unraveling of the mystery. Observe, deduce, reason it out. Don't guess or jump to conclusions; you will probably be wrong.

THE BAFFLE BOOK KEEPS FAITH

The mysteries propounded here are not trick puzzles or riddles with far-fetched answers to be guessed at. There are no trivial "catches" to mislead you. When the book says: "The police established the following as a fact" – the reader may accept that as a fact. The clues to the solution of the mystery are always there; it is for the reader to see them in their significance and to deduce from them in the light of the general situation.

In other words, the *Baffle Book* – unlike many detective stories – keeps faith with the reader by disclosing all the evidence that exists. It does not withhold vital facts for the purpose of baffling you. If the book asks:

"Was it the butler or the chauffeur who committed the crime?" you may assume that one or the other of them did, and you will not find the Answer Section lugging in the hitherto unsuspected ashman as the culprit.

THE IMPORTANCE OF THE SMALL CLUE

The seemingly trifling and insignificant clue may be the most revealing of all, and this is as it should be, for the annals of crime are filled with cases in which brilliant reasoning from faint clues has led to the solution of the mystery.

What could be more admirable than the celebrated feat of M. Goron, Prefect of Police in Paris forty years ago? A wealthy widow was reported missing from her home in the French capital, and foul play was suspected. She had disappeared one afternoon en route to a friend's house where she had promised to spend the night. She had never arrived at her destination. No trace of her could be found. Her nephews were suspected and shadowed. It looked very bad for her favorite nephew, for he stood to profit handsomely by her death.

Several months later a woman's body was found in a Paris park. Such was the condition of the corpse and clothing that not even the widow's servants could say definitely whether it was or was not the body of the widow. The servants ventured that it was, but the nephews said not. The mystery deepened.

Then M. Goron noticed that one of the nephews seemed less perturbed than might have been expected. The famous detective examined again the room of the missing widow and in a drawer found a soiled lace collar with a tiny brown spot on the back. The collar belonged to the widow, and the spot proved to be not blood but hair dye. It had been overlooked at first.

"So, then, your mistress dyed her hair, did she?" M. Goron said to a servant. "And how long had she been doing this?"

"She began about three months before she disappeared," was the reply.

M. Goron again examined the room and took inventory. He found no bottle of hair dye. All other possessions of the widow, except a nightgown, toothbrush, hairbrush and comb, were found in their proper places. The widow had gone, she said, to spend but one night at her friend's – and had never arrived.

"Why should she have taken the hair dye with her for merely an overnight visit?" M. Goron asked himself. She would not have done so, he thought. But she did take it, he reasoned back, and it was precious and essential to her. He deduced that she knew that she would be away longer than she had said.

Why would a rich widow secretly flee with hair dye? For a lover, and a young one, reasoned M. Goron. And he solved the case thereby, for the detective also reasoned that she must have a confidante in one of her nephews, and both were watched. The one upon whom suspicion of murder of his aunt had rested more heavily was caught mailing to her in London a fresh supply of the very same hair dye! It was essential to the widow's appearance in the eyes of the young Frenchman with whom she had fled four months before. The widow had wished to deceive everyone. The corpse was later identified as that of an Italian spy.

That was observation and reasoning triumphant!

Watch for similar subtleties in some of the mysteries to follow. *En garde!* Fifteen crimes have been committed awaiting your solution. What do you deduce?

HOW TO GIVE A BAFFLE PARTY

The Baffle Book grew out of a game. It lends itself well to use at any gathering or party. As devised by two mystery story writers to amuse studio gatherings in New York last winter, the game is sometimes called "Clues" or "Baffling Mysteries." So popular were these concocted mysteries with the players who tracked down the clues, that the best of the problems propounded have been put into book form by the originators. Now anyone can play merely with the aid of this book.

★   ★   ★

PLAYING SIDES
(Requiring two *Baffle Books*)

The host and hostess, or detective captains appointed by them, divide the group into two squads by choosing sides. Each team, armed with a *Baffle Book*, retires to an end of the room. At a given signal each begins work, simultaneously, on a certain mystery problem agreed upon. The team first solving a mystery announces it, without, of course, looking in the Answer Section. If right, the team gets all the credit specified in the book for answering the questions and a bonus of 10 besides (for speed). But if wrong, the team gets no credit and is penalized 5 for jumping to hasty conclusions. In short, the Baffle Book sets a premium on reasoning rather than guessing.

THE ONE-BOOK GAME

It is easy to amuse and baffle your friends by reading a problem to them aloud, slowly and distinctly. Give each player a pencil and paper in case he wants to take a note or two (although this is not necessary); but don't let anyone ask a question until you are through reading the data as given.

For purposes of a game a certain time is allotted for the solution of a problem – make it two or three or five minutes, as you prefer. Of course if everyone is baffled at the end of the first reading, you may reread the problem or parts of it – but only by unanimous consent of those playing. At the end of the allotted time you call a halt and read the solution from the Answer Section. Those who have been baffled and have written nothing down correctly score nothing. Those partly solving get credit for what they have done. Whoever gets the highest total score of the evening wins the title of Sherlock Holmes and is automatically licensed to carry a magnifying glass.

Naturally it always helps a Baffle Party if the host serves shag tobacco. Give a Baffle Party.

P. S.: It is considered the depth of infamy to spread the solutions to the mysteries around the office or neighborhood. Baffle someone with them first.

HINTS FOR SOLVING

Read the text of the mystery or detective problem carefully and consider the questions you are asked at the end of it.

If a diagram of the crime scene, or an illustration of any kind, accompanies the text of the mystery, examine that also for clues; it may give you a clue all by itself or it may tell you something which will further explain a clue in the text.

Sufficient clues from which the answers can be deduced are always to be found in the data given.

Observe, deduce, reason out the solution – don't guess or jump to conclusions.

Don't admit you are baffled until you have spent at least five minutes on the shorter problems, or fifteen minutes apiece on the longer mysteries.

Even when you are baffled, try to answer some of the questions at the end of the problem before you look up the solution in the Answer Section.

To find the Answer Section, shut the book, turn it upside-down, and open again as usual; i.e., the Answer Section is printed upside-down.

For each question rightly answered, you gain certain credits. Mark these down as you go along, under "Credit Score."

NO. I

WHO MURDERED
ELLINGTON BREESE?

Suspicion of guilt of the murder is narrowed down to two
men. Which of them committed the crime and how do you
know it? Examine carefully the following established facts,
then answer the questions put at the end of the problem.

PHILADELPHIA WAS SHOCKED on the morning of
June 5, 1925, by the news of the murder of a distinguished citizen. Ellington Breese, founder and president of the Breese Chemical Works of that city, had
been murdered by poison gas generated in his bedroom during the night.

The police investigation revealed the following per-
tinent facts:

Breese had been found dead in his bed at eight
o'clock in the morning by his Negro servant, who for
years had aroused him at that hour. On the mantel-
piece (there was no fireplace) the police found a glass
flask of about one quart capacity. Its stopper was
missing. It was the kind of glass vessel familiar to any

chemical laboratory. Experts said that one chemical poured upon another would have generated the poison gas immediately, and that diffusion in the room must have followed quickly. Neither on the glass flask nor on other objects were fingerprints found.

Although both windows, screened, had been up eight inches from the bottom, the practically instantaneous effects of the gas had killed every living thing in the bedroom. Breese's pet bullfinch lay dead in its cage. Half a dozen flies and mosquitoes lay dead on the window sills. The dark green shades at the windows were found drawn down nearly to the bottom of the lower window sash, dimming the murder chamber, though the sun shone brightly outside.

The wavering finger of suspicion began to point with equal emphasis at two young men, each of whom was connected with Ellington Breese's business and had had enough laboratory experience to have manufactured the deadly gas.

E. Breese Walters, nephew and only surviving relative of the murdered man, was one suspect. Adam Boardman, Breese's confidential secretary, was the other. Each protested his innocence, each to a degree had an alibi. According to the police investigation, so far as could be determined, both had good records, no debts or entanglements. Both seemed deeply affected by the tragedy.

Neither man seemed capable of committing such a cowardly crime. Yet the police reflected upon the terms of Breese's will, which divided half his estate – about a half million dollars – between the favorite nephew and the devoted employee. The other half of the estate Breese had bequeathed to charity. The terms of the will, drawn five years before, had never been a secret.

Walters and Boardman had maintained cordial but not close relations while in the employ of Breese. Each expressed confidence in the innocence of the other.

The coroner examined the body at 9:30 A.M. and declared that Breese had been dead at least four hours, and possibly for as long as ten hours. The position of the body in the bed indicated to a certainty that death had overtaken Breese while in his bed, to which he had been confined by a slight illness. The police, cherishing a uniform suspicion of Walters and Boardman, decided that they would know the murderer when they knew approximately the hour in which the poison gas was generated in Breese's bedroom.

Boardman, the secretary, had been with Breese until a little after 11:30 P.M. He admitted it, and his leaving the house about a quarter to twelve was confirmed by the testimony of old Mrs. Grew, Breese's boyhood nurse and housekeeper, whose room was near Breese's on the second floor. Boardman had been discussing business matters with his employer, who was laid up in bed convalescing from grippe. He admitted returning to Breese's bedroom for a moment after first leaving it, in order, he said, to secure a briefcase which he had forgotten. At that time, he said, he put out the bedroom light at Breese's request, and closed the door upon leaving. And after leaving Breese's home Boardman went straight to his own. He shared one floor of an old mansion with two other young men. Through the rest of the night and until the body was found his alibi was perfect.

Walters had returned unexpectedly early from Washington, D. C., at one o'clock in the morning. Mrs. Grew heard him enter, came out and spoke to him on the second floor landing and asked if there was anything she might do. Walters said he was not hungry and would go straight to bed. He asked about his uncle's health, heard that Boardman had been there until nearly midnight attending to details of the business, and observed that his uncle must be recovering nicely from his grippe if he could remain at work so late. He went upstairs to his room on the third floor.

Mrs. Grew, who was suffering from rheumatism, returned to her room on the second floor, read for a while, and then went to sleep – not until 2:30 A.M., she believed. From that time until the discovery of the murder, Walters's claim of innocence, like Boardman's, had no support from other testimony than his own.

In short, the police suspected, and their suspicions proved well founded, that if Breese died before midnight it was Boardman who liberated the gas that killed him; and that if Breese died after midnight, then Walters was the slayer of his uncle.

You have now all the evidence from which the Philadelphia police shrewdly fixed the approximate time of the crime and thereby the identity of the murderer.

These are the questions for you to answer:

1. *Which was the slayer?* (Credit 5.)

2. *How did the police deduce it?* (Credit 5.)

Credit Score:

NOTE

When you have answered the questions, turn to page 1 of the Answer Section for the solution, and rate yourself accordingly. The sense or gist of your answers, not the exact phrasing, determines whether or not you have answered rightly.

Rate yourself in the line above marked "Credit Score."

NO. 2

THE EVIDENCE ON THE JAPANNED BOX

THE THEFT OF the celebrated Elgin Emerald occurred under circumstances most embarrassing to Mr. Stephen Lerian, owner of the unique gem. Lerian had been entertaining a house party on his Long Island estate near Westbury. The guests were five in number:

Mr. and Mrs. Archibald Hay;
their niece, Charlotte Grainger;
Colonel Alexander Blue, U.S.A.; and
Mrs. Eleanor Standish, widow of one of Lerian's
    classmates at Harvard.

With what he himself later characterized as inexcusable carelessness, Lerian, the host, had left the emerald in a small black japanned box upon a table in the living room after exhibiting it to the assembled guests one evening. He had been trying for some time to get through a telephone call to Paris, and when finally summoned to the telephone in an adjacent room absentmindedly laid the box on the table and hurried out. When he returned in five minutes, the box was empty.

Assuming that the party was playing a joke on him, Lerian, in mock-serious tones, demanded that the thief step forward. For several minutes he could hardly believe his senses when each of the company, with the utmost emphasis, denied any knowledge of the missing jewel. Judson, the butler, had been in the room during Lerian's absence, as had Ada Gowan, a maid, but these old servants of good character also denied all knowledge of the matter.

For two hours the entire household was in the throes of an excited search on the theory that the jewel had been accidentally lost. But at last Lerian was compelled to face the truth: *someone had taken it.*

To call in the police on so obviously an "inside job" was revolting to Lerian's nature. Absolving everyone from blame in the matter except himself, and insisting that he must have spilled it from the box, he forbade further discussion of the subject, and with remarkable *sang-froid* swept his guests into a game of bridge. It would "turn up," said Lerian.

Afterward, in his own room, with the japanned box before him, Lerian, who is something of an amateur detective, examined the box carefully.

Its surface was highly polished. On the outer rim of the inside of the cover he discovered a remarkably clear thumbprint, which he believed was not his own. He sprinkled it with the white powder used to bring out fingerprints on black surfaces and found it another's. Then he set the box carefully aside.

Lerian knew that none of the company had laid hands on the inside when he had first showed it to them. He reasoned (and subsequent events justified his reasoning) that this must be the thumbprint of the thief. But whose thumbprint? The innocent ones must not suffer suspicion. He resorted to a stratagem.

Lerian put the japanned box carefully away in a wall safe. He then took from his Oriental collection a nest of small black lacquered boxes, whose surfaces were even more telltale than the jewel case. The following morning, Lerian contrived to exhibit to each guest and each servant a different one of the lacquered boxes. To each person separately he told an attractive story of the history of the box and got each to test the strength of the apparently fragile sides by squeezing them between finger and thumb of the left hand; for the thief's thumbprint, as placed on the cover of the case, indicated that a left hand had made it.

Each box, bearing a different thumb mark, Lerian duly secreted in his bureau. When this was done he withdrew to his room and treated the seven small lacquered boxes with white powder. Each, of course, he had subsequently labeled for purposes of identification.

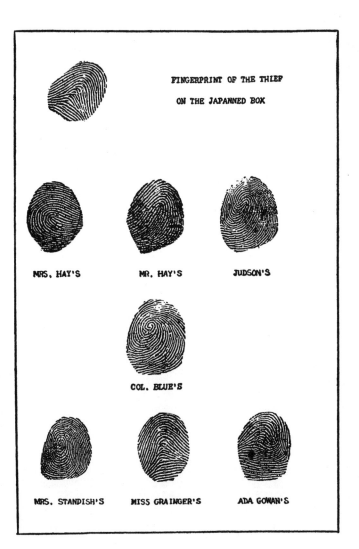

FINGERPRINT OF THE THIEF

ON THE JAPANNED BOX

MRS. HAY'S   MR. HAY'S   JUDSON'S

COL. BLUE'S

MRS. STANDISH'S   MISS GRAINGER'S   ADA GOWAN'S

On the previous page is a reproduction of the thumbprint on the lid of the japanned jewel case, and the thumbprints on the seven lacquered boxes.

What do you deduce? The questions to be answered are:

1. *Did a guest or a servant steal Stephen Lerian's emerald?* (Credit 5.)

2. *Who was the thief?* (Credit 5.)

Credit Score:

NO. 3

THE ELEVATED TRANSIT MYSTERY

This is a three-part mystery. Solve the first part before trying the second, and both before the third – or you will be baffled indeed.

PART I

WHILE SITTING AT THE WINDOW of Cho Sing's Chop Suey Restaurant, at the corner of Tenth Avenue and Forty-eighth Street, early Sunday morning, July 7th, Arthur McGraw and Queenie Walker witnessed the beginning of the celebrated mystery which for eleven days was the sensation of the country. Cho Sing's restaurant occupies the third floor of the building. The table at the window, where the couple sat, is some seven feet below the level of the tracks of the Tenth Avenue Line of the Elevated Transit Company.

As McGraw subsequently testified (corroborated by Miss Walker) they had been watching anxiously to see if the rain was stopping, so that they might leave.

Several times during the previous half hour they had been fascinated by the oncoming roar and rush of the elevated trains, which bore down upon them only to swerve sharply to the left not more than fifteen feet from their window and grind around the curve which marks the turn of the line from Tenth Avenue onto Forty-eighth Street.

At approximately 2:28 A.M. they had just noticed that the shower had stopped and were watching the last car of a train swing around the curve when they were startled to see the figure of a man hurtle downward close to the edge of the elevated road and fall on the sidewalk below. McGraw summoned Cho Sing and several men at neighboring tables and rushed downstairs to render aid.

What they found was even more shocking than they had expected. The man had fallen on his side and had rolled over and over onto a dry spot on the sidewalk which had been protected by an awning. He lay prone, and on turning the man over, the would-be rescuers gasped to find a crimson stain which nearly covered the white starched bosom of his evening-dress shirt. He was dead. Indeed, it was apparent that the man had been dead from stabs even before he struck the sidewalk.

His face was that of a man in his early thirties – dark, handsome, evidently of foreign extraction.

Where the Tenth Avenue Line of the Elevated Transit turns left on Forty-eighth Street. Long arrow at right indicates window where McGraw and Queenie sat. X marks the spot where body struck sidewalk.

Policeman O'Connor, arriving on the scene at 2:33, immediately isolated the body of the man from the gathering crowd and telephoned headquarters at 2:34. Police headquarters telephoned the news to the Elevated Transit Company officials and ordered the train stopped at the nearest station as quickly as it could be done. The records establish that the train was stopped and held at the Forty-second Street Station on Eighth Avenue at 2:36 pending arrival of detectives.

Several detectives from the Forty-fourth Street police station arrived a few minutes later and made a detailed examination of all guards and passengers on the train. The following facts were established:

There was unanimous testimony that no man in evening clothes had ridden in the train since it started from One Hundred and Eightieth Street. William Murphy, transit guard in charge of the platforms connecting the last and middle cars of the train (it was a three-car train), denied that there could have been a stabbing affray on the platform or within either of his cars. He was corroborated by seven reputable witnesses. No testimony gathered revealed any knowledge of the presence of a man answering the description of the dead man. The detectives were baffled.

But since McGraw and Miss Walker, the witnesses of the fall, were certain that they had seen the man fall from the last car, the detectives held Guard Murphy for examination, took the addresses of all fourteen passengers in the rear car, and had the train switched and held. They also picked up "White" Mizzinski, wanted for arson in connection with the Brooklyn apartment house fires. "White" denied any knowledge of the dead man, and his entrance to the train at the Fifty-fourth Street station was substantiated.

The detectives then returned to the scene at Cho Sing's and reexamined the body. They established the following additional details:

Height, 5 feet 6 inches; approximate weight, 140 pounds; cheap quality of cloth in evening clothes. Label of the maker had been cut from clothes. All marks on linen had been removed. No cuff links, wallet, paper, money, or watch were found upon the body.

The patent leather shoes on the victim's feet, soles of which first appeared wet with patches of water, upon careful examination proved to have been waxed. The rain, which had thoroughly soaked the back of the coat and of the trousers, the back of the socks, and even the hair on the back of the head, had been warded off the soles of the shoes. The soles were slippery but not wet. The front of the victim's clothes was dry.

The man had been stabbed twice in the heart, apparently with a long, sharp knife. No fingerprints could be found.

Police Captain Danforth, who arrived at Cho Sing's place soon after the fall of the body, had already established from the testimony of a section track walker (who had inspected the tracks only eight minutes before the tragedy) that the body probably could not have been on the tracks before the arrival of the train which passed the curve at 2:28 A.M.

As is now well known, Captain Danforth, by reasoning solely from the evidence up to then available, reached certain conclusions which were of the greatest importance in the ultimate solution of the mystery. Especially he deduced correctly how the body had come to the sidewalk and what should be done at once.

What do you deduce? These are the questions to be answered:

1. *How came the body to the sidewalk?* (Credit 4.)

2. *Where should the detectives particularly search for clues which might ultimately lead to the catching of the murderer?* (Credit 1.)

Credit Score:

PART II

Have you read and solved the preceding problem – Part I
of "The Elevated Transit Mystery"? It is essential to an
understanding of the part which follows.

IT IS A TRIBUTE TO Captain Danforth's detective
ability in seeking the solution of the Elevated Transit
mystery that he called immediately upon the United
States Government's local Weather Bureau for data to
help him. The body had been seen to fall at approximately 2:28 A.M., and within forty minutes the captain had obtained an official bureau report of the
duration of the rainfall in the uptown district where
the tragedy had been discovered. The report showed
that the shower had burst suddenly at 2:20 A.M. and
had continued for seven minutes, then stopping. At
no time had the rain been merely a drizzle. And there
had been no rain in the city for nineteen hours previous to that time.

With this established fact before him Captain
Danforth would be in a position to consider other
facts which he had ordered obtained. First, a map of
the Elevated Transit Company's Tenth Avenue line,
showing the various stations uptown (i.e., above Cho
Sing's restaurant) and a schedule of Train No. 34
(from which the body had fallen) from its point of origin down to the Forty-eighth Street region. The train,

29

he had ascertained, had been on time all the way down. Captain Danforth had also ordered that the map be marked to show at which points the tracks of the elevated railroad *ran nearest to* the buildings and apartment houses along the seven-mile route. These "zones of suspicion" were three in number. They are indicated by dotted rings on the map which is reproduced on page 31.

Most important of all, Captain Danforth had made a personal examination of the roof of the rear-end car of Train No. 34 immediately after he had deduced that the body probably had fallen from there. The evidence clearly confirmed his conclusion. On the still moist roof, near the very rear of the car, was a dry spot roughly shaped like a cross. Obviously it had been made by the sprawled body of a man whose arms had been extended on either side. It was apparent also that he had lain face down, for a patch of blood stained the dry spot just above the center of it. The victim, it will be recalled, had been stabbed in the heart.

Now the most obvious place from which a body could have been thrown conveniently to a train passing below was the bridge at the One Hundred and Twentieth Street station uptown. This bridge connects the uptown and downtown stations at that point. Captain Danforth had therefore dispatched

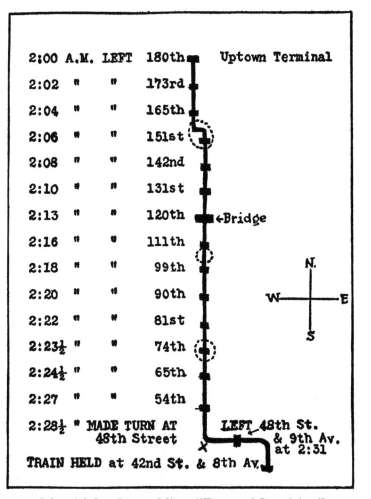

Map of the elevated line. "Zones of Suspicion"
are shown by dotted rings. X marks the spot
where body was seen to fall.

detectives to that station very early in his investigation. Their report, when telephoned to him, proved to be of the greatest importance in connection with the data which he had assembled.

The detectives had found an important witness in the person of Inspector Monahan of the Elevated Transit Company. His night inspection tours (of the signal light system recently installed) customarily brought him to the One Hundred and Twentieth Street station about 2:10 o'clock. Monahan said that he had been smoking a pipe on the bridge while waiting for Train 106 (bound uptown and then not due for eight minutes) when he observed Train 34 come from uptown, stop at the One Hundred and Twentieth Street Station, and pass on downtown. He was absolutely certain that the body could not have been on the roof of the train at that time, else he would have observed it. The police found his testimony convincing, and indeed it may be said that his testimony was confirmed by later discoveries.

Where should further clues be sought? This was the question confronting Captain Danforth at this stage of the investigation. He proceeded to narrow down the three "zones of suspicion" to one in which the murderer must have operated. What conclusion would you have reached from the available data?

The question to be answered is:

To which "zone of suspicion" did Captain Danforth direct the search for further clues to the murderer? (Credit 2.)

Credit Score:

PART III

Have you read and solved the preceding parts of this mystery? Parts I and II should be done before the following third and final part is attempted.

UNDER CAPTAIN DANFORTH'S directions detectives combed the "zone of suspicion" where it seemed most probable that further clues might be found. The Tenth Avenue line of the Elevated Transit Company in this region ran through a section of the city quite mixed in population and in style of buildings. For eight blocks the dingy avenue squeezed itself into a small canyon scarcely thirty-five feet wide in some parts. Drab tenement houses four and five stories high lined the elevated tracks for much of this distance. A hay-and-feed store loft, remnant of the days of the horse; several pool parlors; a Rumanian restaurant (on a third floor); and the "Rooms of the One Hundred and Fifth Street Social Club" (on a fourth floor) were conspicuous among the non-residential apartments on the east side of the avenue.

On the west side of the avenue, besides private dwelling apartments in tenement houses, were to be seen the dingy offices of a Russian newspaper; the gaudy, glaring windows of the Palace Gardens, a dance hall; the Calliope Saxophone School; a storage warehouse seven stories high; and several disreputable-looking armchair lunches and cafeterias. All but the latter had windows which opened above the level of the roofs of the elevated train cars as they passed.

With the exception of the newspaper office, the hay-and-feed store, and the storage warehouse, all the non-residential apartments enumerated had been open late that evening. It was obvious that, once located, the building from which the body had been thrown would have to be searched carefully. One place in particular, Captain Danforth decided, was most suspicious of all. He decided on this place by considering certain facts noted in the early stage of the investigation.

In this place his men found clues which led, some ten days later, to discovery and capture of the murderer. Where would you have searched especially?

The questions to be answered are:

1. *In which building did Captain Danforth's men find clues which ultimately led to the detection of the murderer of the victim whose body was thrown upon the roof of Train* 34*?* (Credit 2.)

2. *How did Captain Danforth deduce that this building rather than any other was worth special investigation?* (Credit 1.)

Credit Score:
    Part I:
    Part II:
    Part III:

NO. 4

THE PROBLEM OF THE BANDIT'S TORN NOTE

This is a simple problem which will serve to prepare for more complicated mysteries to come.

EARLY IN THE EVENING of August 4, 1927, the Chicago police received a tip through the underworld that "Red" Sam Gunther, long suspected as the leader of a band of bank robbers, could be found in the vicinity of a deserted cabin on the outskirts of the city. The stool pigeon's information proved to be correct; Gunther was surrounded by plain-clothes police and was fatally shot as he was about to open fire on his captors.

When surprised, Gunther had just drawn a scrap of paper from his pocket and was in the act of reading it. At the first demand for surrender from the cordon closing in on him, Gunther was seen to jump back, tear the note in fragments and thrust them in his mouth as he drew his automatic pistol. Two detectives fired and the bandit chief collapsed, but not before he had managed to destroy parts of the paper. All but two fragments were chewed beyond legibility. These are shown here. The detectives reconstructed them in order to ascertain the message which Gunther had deemed so important.

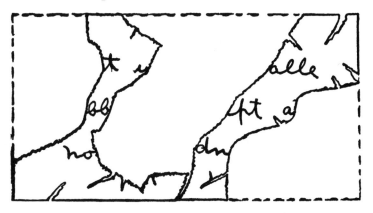

From these fragments the Chicago police were able to deduce the time and place of what proved to be a meeting of the gang. Gunther's death was kept secret, and the police were present at the *rendezvous* with startling success.

Had you been there as a detective, what would you have deduced?

The questions to be answered are:

1. *Where did the gang plan to meet?* (Credit 5.)

2. *When?* (Credit 5.)

Credit Score:

NO. 5

THE SANDY PENINSULA FOOTPRINT MYSTERY

No witnesses to the Sandy Peninsula tragedy were avail-able, but the detectives on the case were able to deduce substantially all that had happened on the lonely beach that bright June afternoon. Footprints told the story. What do they tell you? In this problem the diagram should be studied carefully.

FOUR MILES ACROSS an arm of the sea from the fashionable summer colony of San Serena the Pacific washes on the shores of a sandy peninsula seldom vis-ited by the colonists. Through the center of the nar-row strip runs a macadamized road, skirted on each side by a scrubby hedge of bushes which thrive in slender margins of soil filled in at the time of the building of the road. The road ends at the east in the sea wall. Toward the west it runs with many twistings to the colony of San Serena, thirteen miles away by land.

At five o'clock in the afternoon on the 2nd day of June, Walter Derring, business man and tourist from Los Angeles, stopped his car not far from the peninsula end of the road to examine something which had caught his eye through the bushes. It proved to be the dead body of a man with an ugly bruise on the chin. Derring saw footprints in the sand around the body and immediately comprehended the necessity of an official police investigation before the trails might be confused by footprints of the curious public. He raced his car back to the nearest telephone two miles away and fetched detectives to the spot within twenty minutes.

One of the detectives immediately recognized the dead man as Revington Strang, wealthy Los Angeles sportsman, eccentric, and lately (since separation from his wife) almost a recluse. He had been living in a secluded bungalow near San Serena for several months. An inveterate horseman, his grim figure had frequently been observed of late on the sands and bypaths of the peninsula.

Strang's reputation as a tyrannical and headstrong character had been long since established in southern California, and it had been no surprise to Los Angeles society circles when his wife, the former Dorothy Wilfred, left him soon after the marriage. To Strang's few friends it was no secret that this had cut him deeply.

He had predicted more than once that she would return to him.

The detectives first examined carefully the beach of the peninsula (see the two-page diagram herewith). It had rained most of the morning, and the damp sand showed clear footprint trails. The detectives then established in San Serena that Strang's wife had been staying at the El Principo Inn for several weeks but had been out since noon and had not returned. They also learned from a lighthouse keeper five miles away that a man and a woman had been seen to land on the southwest corner of the peninsula in a canoe "about three o'clock" that afternoon. The keeper, happening to observe them through his binocular glass, could testify to nothing more than that. He had not watched them and had not observed whether or not they departed.

The detectives further established that low tide at the peninsula that afternoon was at 2:40, and that Strang had left his bungalow for a horseback ride about 1:30 that afternoon. Finally they established that Mrs. Strang had been seen almost constantly during her stay at San Serena in the company of a wealthy Easterner. Of him they could learn nothing for the moment except that he was reputed young, handsome, and a former welterweight boxing champion at Yale.

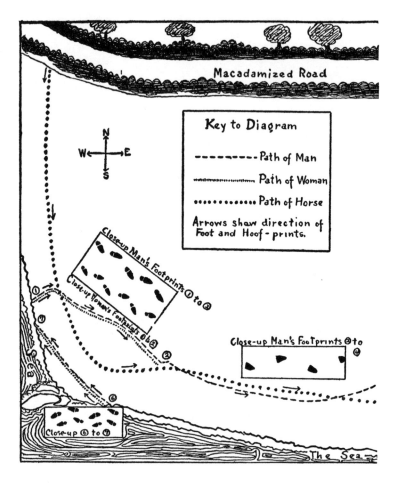

Scene of the Sandy Peninsula tragedy as it

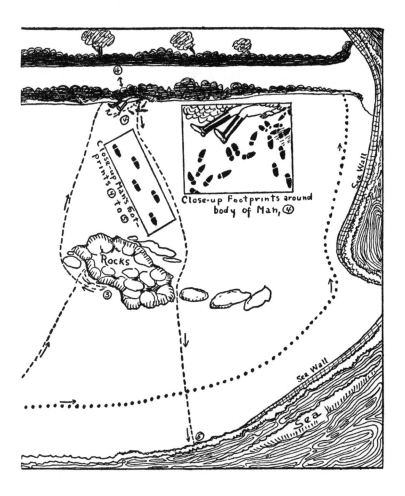

Close-up Man's foot-
prints ④ to ⑤

Close-up Footprints around
body of Man, ④

Rocks

Sea Wall

Sea Wall

Sea

appeared to the detectives at 5:30 P.M.*, June 2nd.*

Within a week the newspapers had printed the full details of the tragedy and its strange aftermath, but let us now suppose that you are the detective on the scene. What would you deduce? How would you reconstruct the tragedy?

The questions to be answered are:

1. *What happened at the spot marked 2 on the diagram?* (Credit 1.)

2. *What did man do between 2 and 3?* (Credit 1.)

3. *What did man do at 3?* (Credit 1.)

4. *What happened on the road near 4?* (Credit 1.)

5. *What became of woman after 4?* (Credit 1.)

6. *What happened near 5?* (Credit 1.)

7. *What happened between 5 and 6?* (Credit 1.)

8. *What happened between* 6 *and* 7*?* (Credit 1.)

9. *What happened after* 7*?* (Credit 1.)

10. *Where, in all probability, did the horse go after the event at* 4*?* (Credit 1.)

Credit Score:

NO. 6

THE CASE OF THE STOLEN VAN DYCK

Can you recognize handwriting through its disguise? Here is an interesting problem in detection.

THE PORTRAIT OF AN OFFICER, Van Dyck's cele-brated painting, since 1907 has been the star of the small but select group of Old Masters in the collection of the Farjeon Memorial Museum of Somerset. On the morning of May 4, 1926, this picture was missing. It had been stolen after the museum was closed to the public (at 5:30) on the afternoon of the 3rd. It had been crudely hacked out of its frame, which was left hanging.

The police investigation conducted by Detective Sergeant Arthur Hurst of the Somerset department could develop no evidences of burglary, nor of the crime having been committed by expert cracksmen or professional thieves. At doors, windows, and skylights Hurst found no signs of forcible entry. Obviously it was one more "inside job."

To recover The Dutch painting obey strickly. I mean it.

Sample of the handwriting of the ransom note.

I used to get $75. a month at the department store but I would

Sample of the handwriting of James Weaver.

I used to be the watchman at McDougall's Dept. Store and I

Sample of the handwriting of John Gregg.

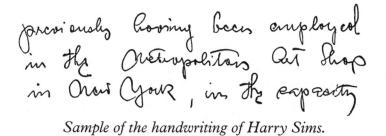

previously having been employed in the Metropolitan Art Shop in New York, in the capacity

Sample of the handwriting of Harry Sims.

At once suspicion focused upon three men having more or less independent access to the museum building. The three were:

JOHN GREGG, night watchman, fifty-six years old, married – who customarily came on duty at 6 P.M., but who on the evening of May 3rd happened to be twenty-one minutes late in reporting.

HARRY SIMS, the day attendant, thirty-nine years old, unmarried – whose duty it was to wait and turn over his keys to Gregg, receiving them again from the watchman at 8:30 A.M. the next day.

JAMES WEAVER, engineer and repair man, forty-nine years old, married, but recently become a widower – who virtually had access to the museum building at all hours, and who had been on duty there on May 3rd as late as 7 P.M., since the weather was raw and the steam-heating plant demanded his attention.

Each denied any knowledge of the theft. The curator, Frederick Jones, was deemed above suspicion.

The Farjeon Collection contained other treasures but the Van Dyck was its richest prize, so famous the world over, it could not be sold by a thief; and the trustees of the museum considered offering a "no questions asked" reward. But this the police vetoed. Detective Hurst said he might be able to trap the guilty one among the three suspects and force him to confess his crime.

But at noon the chairman of the museum's trustees received an astonishing note in a plain envelope, bearing a local postmark, of that day. It was in a handwriting obviously disguised:

To recover the Dutch painting obey strickly. Price is $30,000 cash, otherwise will be destroyed. I mean it. Have someone take the 10:22 train to-morrow morning on the New York Central and ride to Buffalo. Have him stay in the rear car on the back platform and when you see a man beside track waving two small yellow flags throw the money in a bag from the train. The money has got to be in cash, in tens, twenties, fifties and hundreds. Then the painting will be sent back all right. It will come by express prepaid right away, but if the train stops or any police interfere it will be hacked up. I mean it. Maybe you will see the man with the yellow flags soon after the train leaves Somerset and maybe not until near Buffalo. Watch sharp, and remember no tricks.

The trustees decided to take no chances of losing the painting and therefore secretly made preparations for carrying out the instructions of the ransom note. Only after the train had departed the following morning, bearing their representative on the back platform with the money in a bag, was the ransom note revealed to Detective Hurst. The handwriting interested him immensely. He immediately sought samples of the handwritings of the three suspects, and brief search in the records of the museum yielded enough to permit detailed comparison.

Portions of these are reproduced on another page. They were taken from letters applying for positions with the museum several years before the theft of the Van Dyck. A part of the ransom note is also shown.

The writing in the ransom note, the detective reasoned, might be the disguised writing of one of the suspects. Was it? If so, whose? Detective Hurst reached a decision after long study. And the trustees, who had taken due precautions to safeguard their ransom money, reached certain conclusions which checked with Detective Hurst's decision.

The question to be answered is:

Who wrote the ransom note about the stolen Van Dyck? (Credit 10.)

Credit Score:

NO. 7

THE DUNBURY WAYSIDE MYSTERY

HORACE TWICKENHAM, a farmer on the outskirts of Dunbury, arose at dawn one morning in August and, having attended to the stock, drove his cows down the road toward a pasture a quarter of a mile from the house. The road ran between fields bordered with bushes.

About two thirds of the way down, a patch of bright red in the bushes at the south side of the road caught his eye, and on approaching he was appalled to discover the body of a young woman clothed in a flimsy silk dress of brilliant red. She had obviously been hurled into the wayside hedge, for whole bushes had been broken and flattened out by the impact of her body. A single glance at the unusually pretty face of the girl and at her bruised throat told Twickenham that she had been strangled, and strangled by powerful hands. The victim was of medium height and of good figure.

Twickenham, recalling that one should not move the body of a person who might have been murdered (for fear of destroying valuable clues), immediately rushed to the house and telephoned to the Dunbury constable. The constable arrived in less than fifteen minutes, and with Twickenham he proceeded to note in detail the condition of the body and the bushes in the immediate neighborhood.

The constable and Twickenham noted the following facts:

1. The body lay with head to the west and feet to the east. On the right foot was a high-heeled black patent leather slipper. The slipper from the left foot was missing. The light-colored silk stockings were splashed by dew from the bushes. The red dress was also stained in patches a darker red from splashes of dew. The earth around, although soft, showed no footprints.

2. On the soft dirt road one farm-cart track and the tracks of an automobile were distinctly visible. The automobile tracks swerved sharply from the centre of the road to the southern side of the road ten feet east from the point where the body lay, and swerved back to the center of the road some five feet west of that spot.

Charging Twickenham to guard the body and the surrounding scene, the constable rushed to the nearest telephone and gave the news to the Middletown

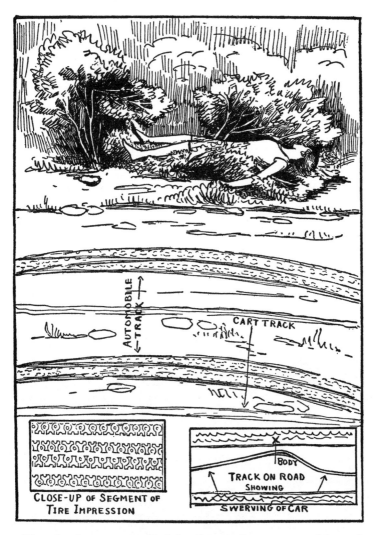

Sketch of scene near Twickenham's farm on outskirts of Dunbury. From photographs made by Middletown Police Department.

police. Middletown was the nearest large town. The police agreed to send an expert medical officer and their detectives. Meanwhile they demanded information which might aid in apprehending the murderer, asking several pointed questions.

Fortunately Constable Barge, although he had never had elaborate training in crime detection, possessed a remarkable native intelligence and was able to answer all of the questions with what proved to be substantial accuracy. Indeed, besides answering their questions, he displayed a bit of initiative in later seeking and finding an important piece of evidence. This eventually established the guilt of the murderer when he was later arrested upon suspicion by the Middletown police at the request of the Dunbury authorities.

Considering the evidence available as described (and do not forget the police sketch), if you had had Constable Barge's responsibilities how would you have answered the questions of the Middletown police?

These are the questions to be answered:

1. *What brand of tires did the automobile have?* (Credit 2.)

2. *Was there more than one man in the car? (Credit 2.)*

3. *Approximately how long had the body been there when discovered?* (Credit 2.)

4. *In which direction was the car traveling?* (Credit 2.)

5. *For what piece of evidence which might have afforded valuable clues would you have a looked?* (Credit 1.)

6. *Where would you have looked for it?* (Credit 1.)

Credit Score:

THE TOLEDO DEATH THREAT CLUE

LATE IN OCTOBER OF LAST YEAR the police of a small Ohio town succeeded in capturing a member of the so-called High School Gang which had been terrorizing motorists of the region by hold-ups and automobile thefts. The prisoner, William O'Connell, eighteen, was held for trial, and the approach of that trial excited unusual attention.

Ten days before the date set the County Prosecutor began to receive threatening letters. The letters afforded no clues to the identity of the sender, but it was assumed that the author was the reputed leader of the gang, "Red" McHarg, a youth of good family who had recently run away from home. Former classmates of McHarg at a neighboring high school were popularly supposed to constitute the gang; it was believed that they alternated their study hours with modern "road agent" work.

On the Friday before the Monday set for O'Connell's trial the prosecutor received a registered letter addressed to him by typewriter. It was postmarked Toledo, Ohio. What purported to be a return address was typed in the left-hand corner of the envelope:

"from Dies Irae, 76 Manassa Street, Toledo, Ohio."

Within was a single sheet of white paper upon which had been pasted, with ordinary mucilage, about a dozen printed words. Only the signature: "D. I." was typed. There was no handwriting on the paper.

What confronted the prosecutor is reproduced here:

If you   go on with the   TRIAL   of   the   captive

you will   NOT   live   to   see   SATURDAY

-- D.I.

The town police communicated with Toledo detectives and found that the return address was a piece of grim and sophomoric humor which might well have been considered characteristic of young McHarg: for 76 Manassa Street was the address of the Toledo morgue. On the heels of this discovery it was learned through the underworld of Toledo that a youth answering McHarg's description was staying at a commercial hotel there.

The town police had no evidence against McHarg for any of the robberies or auto thefts attributed to the gang. They had no proof that he sent the final threatening letter. But they felt sure that the safety of the prosecutor depended upon determining quickly McHarg's guilt or innocence of the sending of the letter. They enlisted the aid of the Toledo police in raiding the room of the man supposed to be McHarg, and among the litter and other articles in the room – torn playing cards, reading matter, scattered poker chips, an empty whisky flask – they found conclusive evidence which positively fastened the guilt upon McHarg.

What would you have deduced from the letter? The question to be answered is:

What did they find there which conclusively fastened the guilt upon McHarg? (Credit 10.)

Credit Score:

NO. 9

THE SCULPTOR'S STUDIO MYSTERY

*Which of the two suspects was guilty of the sculptor's mur-
der? This was the baffling problem which confronted the
Winnetka police. What would you have deduced?*

ON THE MORNING OF November 3, 1922, Reginald
Lamont, famous sculptor, was found dead in his studio on the outskirts of Winnetka, Ill. His skull had
been crushed in by several blows from his own sculptor's mallet which was found not far from his body.
The police were amazed to note that the head of a
large clay statue of Juno in the center of the studio
had been smashed. Fragments of the head which lay
on the floor had been so crushed that they must have
been pounded with a mallet.

Suspicion immediately fastened upon two women.
One was Lamont's wife, a dusky-haired Spanish
woman, thirty-seven years old, who was known to
have posed for the statue of Juno, which Lamont had

*Sketch from police photograph of Lamont's studio made
soon after the murder was discovered.*

been commissioned to do for the Winnetka Park Commission. The other suspect was a well-known model of Scandinavian origin, a statuesque creature who had already received considerable publicity in the tabloids under the descriptive phrase: "the golden beauty who wrecked George Barlow's home" (*à propos* of the celebrated Barlow case in Chicago).

This young woman of twenty-three years, Helga Halverson, was known to have been intimate with the sculptor of late, and admitted having posed for him, two weeks before, for a study of her head. This study was found in the studio.

In many ways it was the most baffling case that had ever confronted the Winnetka police. Both women had seemingly airtight alibis for the afternoon during which the murder must have been committed. Indeed, each claimed not to have been in the studio for a week. Grilling of the suspects yielded no evidence conclusive of the guilt of either, and the officials were beginning to feel baffled – when Detective Coldstream entered the case.

Lamont's body had been discovered at 5 P.M. by James Hogan, elderly handy man who was accustomed to sweep the studio daily. The sculptor's well-appointed workshop (see sketch) and its adjoining living room were in a separate building two miles from the Lamont home. According to Hogan's testimony, both living room and studio had been cleaned carefully at 12:30 P.M. in preparation for the sculptor's arrival to begin work soon after lunch. When questioned by Detective Coldstream, Hogan testified specifically to having removed all ashes and dead embers from the large fireplace, swept it clean, and laid fresh tinder and logs. Hogan lighted the fire, as was his custom, when Lamont arrived at the studio.

According to Hogan, whose testimony was never shaken by the police, Lamont arrived at 1:10. He inquired for telephone messages and was told there had been none. The sculptor dismissed the handy man after a few minutes, requesting him to return at about five o'clock to clean up the studio after the day's work. Hogan returned at this time, discovered the body, and immediately telephoned the police. They instructed him to touch nothing and to lock the studio from the outside, pending the arrival of the detectives.

The first detectives assigned to the case had had the sense to place a large table top over the fireplace to prevent disarrangement of any of the ashes. The fire had died out. It remained for Detective Coldstream to make careful examination and gain from it what clues he could.

Among the warm embers were found the remains of various things which must have been cast into the fire between 1:10 and 5 P.M. These were: part of a carton which had contained Pirate's Delight cigarettes, the sculptor's favorite brand; several sales circulars from artists' supply houses; bits of tinfoil paper supposed to have come from wild cherry lozenges, a half package of which was found in Lamont's pocket; and the perplexing bit of paper which is reproduced here:

To his great credit, Detective Coldstream was able to solve the mysterious crime, deducing both the identity of the guilty one and the motive for the killing with uncanny precision. Throwing the suspect off her guard, he confronted her with the damning evidence. She broke down, and confession followed.

What would you have deduced? The questions to be answered are:

1. *Who murdered Reginald Lamont?* (Credit 2.)

2. *How did Detective Coldstream deduce it?* (Credit 5.)

3. *What probably was the murderess's motive?* (Credit 1.)

4. How did the detective deduce that? (Credit 2.)

Credit Score:

NO. 10

THE BEALS-BLIGH
ANONYMOUS LETTERS

Who was the person that sent two anonymous threatening letters to Sir Chatham Beals-Bligh?

WHEN SIR CHATHAM BEALS-BLIGH, well known in London society, married the rich Miss Millicent Packer of Seattle, Wash., he resolved to give up his life of man-about-town and settle down to more serious pursuits. Accordingly he refurbished the family estate at Tirringham (fifty miles from London) and laid plans to stand for Parliament. There he lived with his bride for nearly a year.

"A one-sided match," said the wiseacres, "he cares less than she does." And so it proved, for when the excitement of superintending the renovations was over, Sir Chatham found time hanging heavy on his hands. His neighbors were dull country squires, and he recalled with envy his former gay life in town. At length, pleading business as necessitating a town visit, he came to London and stopped at his town house.

At the theaters and at his clubs he was hailed as one returning from the dead. Weeks passed into months, and Sir Chatham found it hard to return to his wife and the life at Tirringham. Indeed it soon became common gossip about town that Sir Chatham had resumed relations with a certain Austrian baroness, at whose home before his marriage he had been seen frequently.

To Sir Chatham's valet, Hobbs, this was a most unsatisfactory state of affairs, for he had recently become engaged to Suzette, Lady Beals-Bligh's young and charming French maid. And Hobbs, being a middle-aged and somewhat bald man, was afraid that in his continued absence Suzette might yield to the attractions of one of the younger servants.

At 10 A.M. one day in the third month of his absence from Tirringham, while telephoning to his wife at the Tirringham mansion, Sir Chatham was surprised to hear Lady Beals-Bligh announce her intention of coming to town the following day. It was clear to Sir Chatham that she was not to be wheedled out of carrying through the trip, and late that afternoon he set out on a last evening of freedom. Hobbs, who had asked for the evening off, departed from the house a few minutes later.

Sir Chatham returned shortly after midnight. Glancing, through habit, at the hall table where his mail was left by the servants in his absence from the house, he noticed a long envelope on which his name and address were written in crude block letters, all capitals. He tore open the envelope and with surprise and anger read the following unsigned note. Hand printed, it gave Sir Chatham no clue to the identity of the sender:

ALL YOUR PLANS WILL BE RUINED IF YOU CONTINUE THIS DISHONORABLE AFFAIR, SINCE I HAVE INCONTROVERTABLE PROOF, AND WILL USE IT WHERE IT WILL DO THE MOST HARM, IF IT IS NECESSARY.

The letter was postmarked 10:30 A.M. of that day, Paddington Station, London. Summoning the butler from his bed, Sir Chatham learned that it had arrived in the mail a few minutes after his departure from the house.

Sir Chatham smoked his pipe furiously before the fire. Who was dipping into his affairs? Was it blackmail? Could Hobbs be a traitor? He rang for the valet, but the housekeeper said Hobbs was still out.

At any rate, Sir Chatham reasoned, Hobbs could not have mailed the letter at the Paddington Station just before 10:30 that morning, for he had attended Sir Chatham constantly from 7:30 until noon. And Sir Chatham knew that the mailboxes at Paddington were cleared every half hour. "Hobbs could not have left the house long enough to have mailed the letter there

– not Hobbs, of all persons," Sir Chatham concluded, for the valet had been devoted to him for seven years.

Fifteen minutes later Hobbs arrived, out of breath from hurrying. He explained that he had spent the evening at Hilton, a suburb of London. He said he had missed the last train and had to return by motor bus. Sir Chatham forbore to question him that night, but decided to watch him carefully.

The following morning Sir Chatham was amazed to receive, in the first delivery of the mail, another envelope of the same type, addressed in hand-printed block letters which resembled those in the anonymous note of the day before. But minute examination showed clearly that they were not from the same hand; the second note was only a fair imitation of the first. Its message was short:

WHAT I MEAN IS, I WILL TELL YOUR WIFE IF IT DOES NOT STOP.

To his astonishment, the letter was postmarked Hilton, the previous evening – Hilton, the very suburb where Hobbs had missed his train the night before. In a sudden rage Sir Chatham Beals-Bligh accused the valet of having sent the letters and confronted him with both. Hobbs was shocked and protested in the most violent terms that he was innocent and specifically that he had no knowledge of the existence of the letters until they were laid before him. He said that he had gone alone to Hilton, where he often went on his evenings off, when in London, to play cards with a friend, Raoul Gascoigne, keeper of the well-known French tavern at Hilton.

Sir Chatham was deeply affected by Hobbs's outburst, and, upon thinking it over, regretted his accusations. He reasoned that the valet surely could not have been so great a fool as to have told him on the previous evening that he had been at Hilton if he had had knowledge that the second letter would bear the Hilton postmark. Sir Chatham was baffled.

At noon Lady Beals-Bligh and her maid Suzette arrived at the town house. Alone in their apartment, his wife greeted him so affectionately that Sir Chatham impulsively decided upon a daring step. In fear that the anonymous threat might be carried out, he poured out his heart to his wife, telling her of the letters, making a clean breast of his relations with the baroness, and throwing himself on his wife's mercy. He gave assurances that he loved only her and that she need never fear a similar "indiscretion," which he said he deeply repented.

Lady Beals-Bligh received his confession in silence, and then without a word rose and left the room. An hour later she and her maid departed in a cab with her luggage.

Angered alternately at his confession and the rejection of it by his wife, Sir Chatham summoned his counsellor at law, an old friend, and laid the anonymous letters before him with instructions that the identity of the sender be discovered at all costs. He also gave instructions that handwriting experts be called on the case. A searching investigation was immediately requested of a private detective, former Inspector Givott, quondam anonymous letter expert of Scotland Yard. The counsellor at law promised a full report to Sir Chatham within a few days.

The following morning, while fully expecting that his wife's next communication would be through her solicitor, Sir Chatham was amazed to receive a letter postmarked Tirringham. It was an affectionate and philosophical letter from his wife, written the night before; it closed with this paragraph:

. . . and so, Chat, my dear, though at first I thought I could never forgive you, especially when you referred to your unfaithfulness as "an indiscretion," I do not think that God ever intended us to seperate, and if you really mean what you said today, come home and we will begin a new life, for I have been very unhappy since I left London, just as I know you have been since I went away – haven't you, darling?

Ever your loving wife,
MILLICENT.

With an unaccustomed alacrity and cheerfulness, Hobbs thought, Sir Chatham Beals-Bligh ordered the immediate packing of his bags and announced the welcome news that they were to leave for Tirringham. Sir Chatham called at the office of his counsellor and showed him the forgiveness letter. He placed a sum at the disposal of the investigating detective and ordered the result of the search to be forwarded to him at Tirringham. And he and Hobbs departed.

Three days later Sir Chatham's counsellor replied that the private detective could make no headway on the case whatever. And he added the opinion that unless annoyed by further anonymous letters, Sir Chatham might just as well let the matter rest.

And Sir Chatham did just that.

What do you make of the mystery? The questions to be answered are:

1. *Who sent the anonymous letters?* (Credit 2.)

2. *How is the sender's identity logically deduced?* (Credit 5.)

3. *Was there an accomplice to the act? (Credit 3.)*

Credit Score:

MESSER BELLINI'S REPORT TO THE DOGE

A fascinating problem in crime detection is to be found in the Twelfth Century document recently authenticated by Professor Paolo Capelli of the University of Milan, which deals with the murder of one Giacomo Geronimo, evidently a favorite adviser of the Doge (or Duke) of Venice in the latter part of the century. The sketch and the portions of the text of the report printed here are taken from the old English translation, known since 1530 and probably of earlier origin.
For all practical purposes the version is identical with the Capelli translation.

Being the report of Messer Marco Bellini Made Privately to His Excellency, The Worshipful Aberno Arbasini, God's Knight of the Cross and Reverend Doge of Venice, in the Year of Our Lord 1189, on the Third of the Month December:

WORSHIPFUL SIR:
Mindful of Your Excellency's most gracious com-

mand, your servant, I, have caused to be inquired into the untimely and abominable death of Your Excellency's quondam Minister and true friend (God Rest His Soul!), the valiant Geronimo, for that Your Excellency hath suspicion that his death was caused not by his own hand as some have it but by the cunning encompassment of his enemies. And mindful of Your Excellency's command I have set aside the reports of others of the household who made pretence of inquiries, and have discovered now the solemn truth of this fearsome deed.

Know, Worshipful Sir, that it was by the hand of the Cavaliere himself that the brave Geronimo was snared to his death, and in a villainous, cunning and subtile manner which, if it be not disclosed, will imperil all citizens of the Republic upon whom this Torcello's jealousy and evil spirit falls. For it was a dreadful deed and of the guiltiness of the Cavaliere Torcello there can be no longer doubt, seeing the repute of my informants and the dove-tailing of their separate testimonies. Which testimonies are, to wit:

The oath of Fernando, the poetaster, whose wretched rhymes could come only from a simple mind which could not be guileful if it would:

"For the Worshipful Messer Bellini, I swear, that I was guest at the dinner of the Cavaliere Torcello whereat the valiant Geronimo met his death, and have suspicions that it was from the wine then and there drunk that he died and not from the lavendered sugar which he carried and ate of custom, which latter was first reported and is widely cherished by the populace. And my reasons for this are, namely: that I too ate of the Worshipful Geronimo's lavendered sugar freely when he offered me his box on the terrace of the Cavaliere's *palazzo*, we having entered together, and naught of any harm came to me therefrom.

"So that those who say that the valiant Geronimo died from sugar which he alone did eat, do err, forasmuch as I also ate. And those who say that it could not have been from the wine drunk, forasmuch as the Cavaliere poured for all guests from the same pitcher, they also err, since of this pitcher something happened of which none wot save I and the girl Baptista. But it is not clear in my head, for I was much drunk and enamored of the girl Baptista as well. Yet she can tell without doubt, for it was she who blew into the pitcher and it was then that the bubble came and we were affrighted and left the table. No more will I say, but she can tell and will, since the Cavaliere but last week cast her off."

No more, Your Excellency, could I gain from this Fernando, he being a timid one and easily affrighted. Yet look upon the testimony of Baptista, the harlot, a shrewd and honest girl who would be a dancer:

The oath of Baptista Vittore, late of the household of the Cavaliere Calergi Torcello:

"For the Worshipful Messer Bellini, I swear, that I was bidden to the dinner whereat the valiant Geronimo met his death, being told by my master, the Cavaliere, to attend and observe the manners of the gentles that I might learn from them, though if what I saw that night amongst the ladies of Venice be graces, may I never be a lady, since I know sin when I see it as well as the next.

"And that the valiant Geronimo was poisoned to his death I do not doubt, and all from a pitcher bewitched (God Save the Mark!) from the hands of the Cavaliere himself. And the events fell out in this way: that a dozen of company was present and the Cavaliere poured a precious wine from a pitcher and made a great show of serving all from the same pitcher and did it ever with his own hands. And all drank and were warmed and thereafter for long all drank from cups ever refilled from the Cavaliere's pitcher, and this ever and anon filled from a wineskin. And all made merry and called each other friend, and I did watch the Cavaliere closely when he would pour for Geronimo and nothing did he put stealthily in Geronimo's cup or in the pitcher, for all were openly looking.

"Yet soon after a pouring, mayhap the twelfth or the twentieth, I know not which, and whilst the merriment was at its height, I beheld the valiant Geronimo clutch at his stomach, and several friends bore him to another room, but all thought him drunk and that was all, for much wine had been drunk, nor did I think aught amiss. And the Cavaliere made great ado to ease the pain of the valiant Geronimo and swore that it was a pity that a man should mix lavendered sugar with his drinking as Geronimo had done.

"And at that time, when the Cavaliere was in the next room, and all the others drunk and fondling, this Fernando, the rhymester, was pawing at me and I cried to mock him:

Sketch of the wine pitcher used by the Cavaliere Torccello as described in Messer Bellini's report to the Doge.

76

" 'Nay, I will not kiss thee! I will kiss my own true love which is this wine-pitcher!'

"And then, for a jest, I leaned to the pitcher standing on the table and made as if to kiss its lip whence the wine issued, but Fernando at this moment tugging my arm, I could not reach it with my lips, but falling somewhat short I blew under the lip of the pitcher, laughing loudly.

"And then a strange thing happened, for even as I blew, a great glistening dark bubble came on the side of the pitcher, swelling out from one of the blossoms which adorned the vessel near to the handle of it. And then it burst and, from whence it had come, a black drop oozed. And Fernando and I were amazed and we knew that the pitcher was bewitched, for the wine therein was not of that hue but a palish red. And I broke away from the rhymester and fled from the room, nor will I go again to the Torcello *palazzo* though the whole college of cardinals go with me, since I mistrust the Cavaliere and his cunning smiles. For ere I fled to my room Geronimo had died in agony."

And now, Worshipful Sir, comes that which binds the deed to this smiling villain whose ill-will we have had cause enough to guess. For, my suspicions aroused, I have covertly sought from a servant of the Cavalier's household a further description of this strange pitcher and . . .

To quote further from Messer Bellini's report would reveal to the reader too plainly the explanation of the mystery which had baffled the Doge's investigator. How do you explain the death of Giacomo Geronimo, and the Venetian wine pitcher? How came the dark bubble and what did it mean?

On page 76 is reproduced a sketch of the celebrated vessel, the first known of its kind. The sketch was drawn from the painting accompanying the manuscript of Messer Marco Bellini's report. Examine it carefully and answer the following questions:

1. *How was Torcello able to single out Geronimo from the other guests in administering the poison?* (Credit 5.)

2. *What probably would have happened to Baptista if she had helped herself to wine?* (Credit 2.)

3. *Why was the fretwork of the pitcher* open *everywhere except near the lip of the pitcher?* (Credit 3.)

Credit Score:

NO. 12

THE MYSTERY OF THE MURDERED PHYSICIAN

Was Dr. Brett's murderer a man or a woman? Even this much the Arden police never determined. But Inspector Marquard of Scotland Yard, on his recent visit here, revived interest in this celebrated, unsolved mystery by his statement that the sex of the murderer was conclusively indicated by evidence available from the very first.
What is your opinion?

DR. WINTHROP BRETT, of Arden, it will be recalled, was among the first of American physicians to journey to Vienna for tutelage when the fame of Freud began spreading through knowing medical circles early in the century. By 1926 the Arden psychoanalyst had fairly skimmed the cream of the wealthy, select patronage in his region, and had amassed a fortune so large that cynical ones whispered talk of blackmail as an adjunct to his specialty. Among the newspaper men of Arden, the physician's now famous "little green books" had

79

long been a by-word. To city editors, at least, his murder was not the most unexpected of things. It was common gossip among them that there were a half dozen men or women who might have had sufficient motive to commit the crime.

The first notice of the murder of Dr. Brett came from Wilkins, the physician's valet, who telephoned the police at 6:05 P.M. in the greatest excitement. (It was on November twenty-second, a chilly day.) He said that he had just returned from an afternoon off and had found his employer shot dead in the private study of his bachelor apartment. The police ordered Wilkins to touch nothing in the apartment pending the arrival of detectives.

Fifteen minutes later, police entered the private study in the apartment. Brett's body was lying on its left side, back against the wall, directly below the wall safe. The victim had been shot twice from a .25 caliber automatic. One bullet had entered the abdomen; the other, the right lung. The lung wound had caused a hemorrhage. A great crimson stain of blood covered the entire front of the physician's gray, double-breasted coat from collar to waist and extended to the heavy grayish-blue rug on the floor.

Medical examination later revealed that he must have been dead for more than an hour. It was observed that although the pockets of the physician's clothes had been rummaged, his gold watch and $72 in small bills were untouched. His keys, however, were missing and were never found.

The wall safe, 5 feet from the floor, below which the physician's body was found had been opened – undoubtedly with keys removed from the dead man's pocket, for it had not been forced. Examination revealed that a small black steel box had been removed and replaced. From this black steel box the small green leather-covered books had been taken, according to the deductions of the police. It was within these books that Dr. Brett kept many of his private case records, and it was presumed (and never has been disproved) that they rested within the steel box as usual on the day of the murder.

The alibi of Wilkins, the valet, from 2:30 that afternoon until he telephoned the police, was early established by the detectives and cannot be questioned. In fact, it should be said that no justifiable suspicion of Wilkins, either as a principal or as an accomplice in the crime, has ever been established by any evidence, and it may be assumed that Wilkins told everything that he knew.

The detailed examination of Wilkins brought out the interesting fact that the physician had made an appointment for three o'clock that afternoon with a person who had telephoned at about one o'clock. Wilkins's testimony follows:

"The doctor didn't go to his office downtown on Tuesdays, so he was home here this morning. He went out for lunch at twelve and returned just before one. I was in the private study putting some books in the closet for him when his private telephone rang. That is the one on his desk. It is not connected with the apartment switchboard.

"He was sitting at the desk and he answered it himself. He didn't greet anyone; he wasn't surprised or angry. He was very matter-of-fact, and I never noticed *what* he said except when he called me and said:

"'Wilkins, you may have the afternoon off until six!'

"The doctor sometimes said that to me suddenly, and I was always glad to go whenever the opportunity came. He was still holding the wire when he said that to me. Yes, I am quite sure he resumed conversation on the 'phone *after* saying that to me, for when I came out of the closet later, I remember him laying down the 'phone. Then he said:

"'You can go at 2:30, Wilkins. I have an appointment for three and I shall be dressing for dinner at eight. You may stay away until six.'

"So I left him then and didn't get back till after six. I always followed orders with Dr. Brett. He often had confidential appointments with lots of people, you understand, and I always followed orders exactly."

The detectives proceeded with a minute examination of the private study, but they found no finger-prints. The highly polished surface of the black steel box, the wall-safe door, and the doctor's black wallet – all these, which must have been examined and touched by the murderer – had been wiped clean of fingerprints, as if with a wet cloth.

A damp towel was found over the handle of the door leading into the bathroom adjoining. It was also noted that the cold water at the bathroom wash basin was still running (about one quarter on). Wilkins testified that it was thus when he first inspected the apartment at 6:05. In this he was corroborated by the Negro elevator operator of the apartment building, who had answered Wilkins's startled cry for help upon discovering the tragedy.

But what most attracted the attention of the police was the position of the doctor's body as it lay, back against the wall, on the floor below the wall safe. It was apparent that the murderer would have been compelled to reach over the body to open the wall safe. On the desk lay a novel – as if the physician had been reading when his visitor entered.

On the floor near one of the radiators of the room a single sheet of newspaper was found – the back page of that morning's *Arden Argus*. The remainder of the paper lay on a table near by. The detectives noted that a part of the single sheet of newspaper was shriveled,

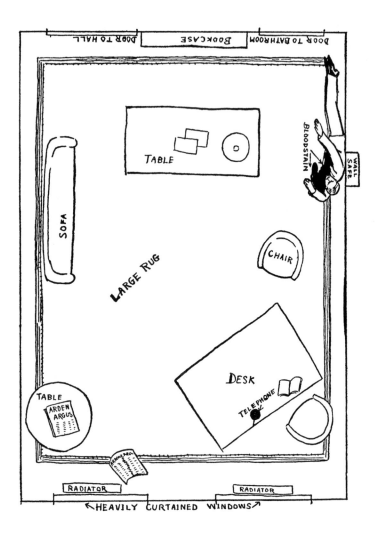

Police diagram of Dr. Brett's private study, showing where the body of the murdered physician was found. (Courtesy, Arden Police Commissioner Treadwell.)

as though it had been previously wet. The shriveled portion ran down the middle of the paper almost from top to bottom, for a little more than a column's width. When questioned, Wilkins, the valet, was certain that the *Argus* was complete and untorn on the table when he left at 2:30.

Scrupulous examination of the physician's apartment yielded no further clues. Nothing of importance was gleaned from the neighboring apartments, from the elevator operator, or from the apartment switchboard operator. No one remembered either a man or a woman calling at the Brett apartment – either going or coming – at any time during the afternoon. This was not extraordinary, however, for the apartment was on the ground floor and it was not necessary to pass the elevator operators or switchboard operator in order to ring the doctor's bell and gain entrance. No shots had been heard.

The net deductions of the Arden police were as follows; and since Inspector Marquard agrees they may be assumed correct.

1. The murderer came by appointment at three o'clock, stayed for an hour or more, and then shot the physician.

2. The murderer robbed the wall safe and erased the fingerprints *without haste*, apparently secure in the

knowledge that the valet, Wilkins, would not return for some time and that disturbance from anyone else was a remote possibility.

The Arden police, at the time, held it impossible to do more than guess at the sex of the murderer. But Inspector Marquard says that evidence affording clues to the murderer's *actions* in the apartment *after* the shooting, proves conclusively the sex of the murderer.

What do you deduce? Don't guess; reason it out. The questions to be answered are:

1. *Was a man or a woman the murderer of Dr. Brett?* (Credit 1.)

2. *What conclusively proves the sex of the murderer?* (Credit 9.)

Credit Score:

NO. 13

THE AFFAIR OF THE FRENCH SPY

During the World War many subtle brains were devoted to originating secret forms of communication, and also to detecting the new codes and ciphers used for communication by the enemy. An episode illustrating the keenness of the secret agents in this "underground combat" between espionage and counter espionage occurred in Switzerland. It presents an interesting problem.

A CERTAIN MLLE G., an agent of the French, had been assigned to the French counter espionage service; that is, to the branch of the Secret Service which spies upon spies. In Berne, in Zurich, and Geneva, Mlle G. posed so successfully as a Swiss lady that she succeeded in gaining the confidence of German espionage agents. These sought to engage her as a German agent to spy upon the French. For her, this was extraordinary luck; she accepted their offer, and her French superiors were delighted. Her reports to the

French became increasingly valuable since she was now gaining important information from the Germans while pretending to serve them.

One day, however, the French counter espionage headquarters was shocked to learn through Belgian sources that some one of their trusted agents on the French espionage payroll had proved treacherous to them and was in reality serving German agents – that is, had become a double spy and was deceiving them, even as Mlle G., their agent, was a double spy deceiving the German adversary.

The French immediately grew anxious to discover the identity of this treacherous agent so that he might be arrested at once. They secretly informed Mlle G. of the situation and ordered her to lose no time in seeking this essential information, without, however, in any way betraying herself to the German agents in Switzerland with whom she was now daily associating.

By surreptitious examination of documents in the official files of her German associates, Mlle G. managed to learn the identity of the treacherous spy just an hour before she was due to leave Berne on an important commission for her German employers. If she were to get her important information to her French employers quickly enough for them to seize the traitor, it was necessary that she do so before the hour was up, for after that she would be constantly in

Mlle. G. as she awaited her confederate in the lobby of the hotel.

the company of the Germans. She could not telegraph the message, for she knew that the telegraph offices were honeycombed with espionage agents of all countries, and if any of them decoded the message it might lead to her own discovery. Mail would be too late.

There was one chance: fortunately, Mlle G. had arranged an appointment in her hotel lobby with one of her French confederates in Berne so that she might give him, if necessary, the latest information before she left. But she felt certain that she and her visitors were watched at all times, so it had been arranged that her confederate should take a seat near her in the hotel lobby but not take the initiative in addressing her.

In short, Mlle G. was faced with the difficult problem of conveying a vital message upon very short notice to a confederate who could be near her and watch her but with whom she might not dare to hold conversation. Indeed, in view of the certain presence in the lobby of German agents who might be watching her closely, she knew that she must not be seen nodding significantly, signaling by hand, or doing anything which might arouse their suspicions.

In spite of the difficulties confronting her, Mlle G. acquainted her confederate with the identity of the treacherous French spy and without attracting attention. And within ten hours the spy was under arrest.

How did she do it? The accompanying sketch shows Mlle G. as she sat in the main salon of a well known hotel in Berne. She stayed there for only five minutes, reading a book. Her confederate seated near her got the communication, yet there was no talk between them. She returned to her room unsuspected.

The questions to be answered are:

1. *How did Mlle G. communicate the message to her confederate?* (Credit 7.)

2. *What was the text of the message?* (Credit 3.)

Credit Score:

NO. 14

THE KIDNAPPING OF DR. ADAIR

The kidnapping of Dr. Thomas Jefferson Adair, professor of Latin Literature at Robertson College, New York City, must always rank with the most bizarre incidents in the annals of American crime. For some years now the police have withheld details in the hope that Baldassare, the brains of the singular scheme, would be caught. As a result the public has always been ignorant of the exact motive for the kidnapping. Why Dr. Adair was snatched from the calm routine of his sheltered life and whither he was taken you will probably deduce. But it is not an easy problem.

THE FEW ESTABLISHED FACTS in the case are well summarized in Dr. Adair's own naïve account of his curious adventures, which he submitted as a private report to the president of his college soon after his return.

"... I am unable to say whether or not I would be able to recognize my captors in the event of encountering them again. I cannot positively testify that I ever did see them; but if I did, I saw them but once.

"Some ten days before the Friday of my disappearance I chanced to be sitting in the lobby of the Imperial Inn on the outskirts of the campus when I suddenly became aware of a pair of men upon a couch across the aisle some fifteen feet away. I was first attracted by a tense, suppressed cry: 'Good God, *Milliken!*' This came from the larger of the two, a powerful, tallish individual, of perhaps forty-five years, with a florid face, brown hair, and brown moustache. His companion, who I judged must be named Milliken – a small, keen-eyed, dark-complexioned man, with a smooth-shaven face – half started from his seat, staring toward me with the most astonished expression.

"There was something so startling about the manner in which both men stared in my direction that I turned to look behind me to see what could possibly have so excited them. To my surprise there was no one in the vicinity, and I realized that I must be the object of their attention. By the time I had turned around again the smaller man had seized his tall companion by the arm and was impelling him toward the center of the crowded part of the lobby. They glanced back, however, several times, evidently greatly agitated. I was completely nonplussed and was about to allow myself to indicate some resentment, when, with a final glance, the smaller one fairly shoved his companion around the corner of a column, and they disappeared.

"I recall narrating the incident to Professor Mendham on our walk through the campus a few minutes later, but until the evening of my capture I confess that I never gave it another thought.

"It was a Friday morning. I was returning from the seminar at about ten o'clock when the assault took place. I was passing the bushes near the observatory (perhaps the loneliest spot on the campus) when I was seized by strong hands, a bandage fastened over my eyes, and a sponge pressed upon my face. When I came to, I was lying flat on my back on some sort of cot or stretcher in what I judged to be a large motor van. I was blindfolded, bound, and gagged.

"It was then, as I was coming out of my coma, that I heard the voice which I believe was that of the tall, florid faced man encountered in the lobby of the inn. He was talking to another; both were in the driver's seat in the front of the vehicle. At the very outset, I was relieved to learn that my captors intended no bodily harm to me. The man whom I guessed to be the tall, florid fellow said:

"'I won't stand for any tricks. The old boy has got to be well kept and no harm come to him – not even let him get sick – or I am *off* of it, Lester."

"'Fool,' said 'Lester' in a crisp, masterful voice,

'don't you suppose I realize that? You can take care of him yourself, good care of him; *of course* nothing must happen to him, after all this trouble. But that's all you have to do – you leave the rest to me.'

"The other (anxiously): 'But are you sure it's airtight?'

" 'Certainly, leave it to me. Nobody around here has seen him in twenty years, I told you.'

" 'Well, Lester, you're a clever man, and it's worth trying for. But–'

" 'But what?' demanded the one addressed as Lester.

" 'Well, you don't think there's any chance that *he* has left there, do you, and come *here* and heard about things?'

" 'Now I ask you *what* chance,' was the reply. 'How often did a ship touch in the four years we were there? Just three times, Rory, remember that. No chance in the world! Besides *he liked* it there. Or he may be dead now for all we know. Don't get in such a blue funk.'

"At this point the roar of a passing motor drowned out their conversation, but presently the tall one said in a pleading voice:

" 'But he ain't tall enough, Lester.'

"To which his companion replied in a mysterious way:

" 'My dear fellow, there are always boxes.'

95

"A moment's silence, then, the other:

" 'Lord, Lester, but you're a clever one.' "

Much of Dr. Adair's account may be summarized as follows: He was told politely but firmly to make no resistance, to ask no questions, to follow instructions, and to make no sound without permission. He was guaranteed good treatment, and indeed he experienced it throughout the duration of his captivity. Within a few minutes of recovering his senses and hearing the first conversation between his captors, the vehicle in which the Doctor was carried rolled onto what he supposed to be a ferryboat. He smelled salt sea air. After what he judged to be ten or fifteen minutes the car rolled onto land again.

About three hours later the car evidently passed through a large city since Dr. Adair acutely noted the heavy rumble of passing traffic, which endured for about a half hour. At several traffic stops he heard newsboys shouting *Bulletin*, but beyond this he heard no identifying sounds. Another three hours of travel elapsed – then another rumble of heavier traffic and boys crying *Sun*. He guessed another city, but did not know which.

They proceeded. After an hour and a half he sensed their entrance into a third city, but here the traffic rumble was much lighter and Dr. Adair distinctly noted the passage of the car around many curves because of the frequent sideway slides of his cot within the vehicle. He also noticed that the car seemed to be running with fewer bumps than at any time previously on the trip.

After about ten or fifteen minutes of travel within this city the car stopped and he was ushered into a building. He was still blindfolded. He was then given food and put to bed in what he sensed was a second floor bedroom of an old house. He heard nothing more informative that night.

The next morning after breakfast, his captors ordered him to don a dressing gown furnished by "Lester." The blindfold was removed, a revolver placed threatfully against his back and whispered orders given to him. He was forced to stand on a short wooden box close to a front window.

"I had no choice but to obey," the Doctor writes, "and I soon comprehended that I was being required to address a trio of men standing upon the porch below. In my agitation I had little opportunity to fix the details of the scene in my mind. They were conventional-appearing individuals of the business type – well dressed. They bowed very cordially to me – indeed, almost obsequiously, I thought – as if they were anxious to have my favor. They stood with hats removed while I made the following hesitant remarks whispered to me by the small man who had been addressed by his comrade as 'Lester.'

"'Gentlemen, good-morning! I must apologize to you for not joining personally in the conference, but the fact is that Dr. Villard here' – and at this point my arm was pushed up from behind so that my hand rested upon the shoulder of the larger fellow who stood beside me, quite visible in the window – 'Dr. Villard insists that my condition will not permit leaving my room. However, this need not delay matters' – and at this the faces of my auditors showed considerable satisfaction.

"'If you will be good enough to wait in the parlor below, my attorney, Mr. Devore, will confer with you on the details as agreed, and he will bring me the papers for signature. I see no reason why we cannot settle the matter within a very few minutes.'

"This seemed to please the men below, and they bowed cordial assent as I withdrew from the window. I was immediately blindfolded again without having seen the faces of my captors, and bound in bed. The two men then hurried from the room. I waited momentarily for the coming of the papers which I supposed I would be compelled to sign, but strange to say none were ever brought to me. About a half-hour later a door slammed downstairs and the two returned. With a goodwill that they could scarcely conceal they proceeded to thank me for my 'good coöperation,' albeit enforced. Indeed, the one who was addressed as 'Lester' was quite surprisingly cordial in tone. He said with what I judged was a feeling of relief:

"'My dear Doctor, you have no idea how you have furthered the ends of justice by doing as we asked you to do without any attempt to escape. Some day you will be well rewarded for this. It is impossible to explain now, but you may be sure we shall not forget you. Perhaps you can never forgive us for our unconventional manner of seeking your help. But I repeat that some day you will be very glad that we gave you the opportunity. We will now return you to the college.'

"And with that my captors shut off any questioning and we departed as suddenly as we had arrived, this time, however, leaving by what I judged must be a side entrance rather than the front door. I have always believed that this was done to avoid the suspicious sight of a blindfolded man being led into an automobile at the curb in bright daylight. We rolled out of what was possibly an alley and then down onto a smooth pavement.

"From then on for some seven or eight hours our journey was uneventful. Soon after dark I was ordered to step from the car and was led perhaps a hundred yards over a field. My blindfold was removed. I was thanked again and warned to say nothing. A small roll of bills was placed in my hand. 'Lester' ordered me to remain without turning for several minutes.

" 'Then follow the road into Jersey City, Doctor,' he said. 'It's not more than a couple of miles. You'll see the lights. Good-bye.'

"And with that I was left alone. I heard the car speed away and a few minutes later turned to find myself, as he had said, near a road which led toward a mass of lights. Beyond loomed the familiar lights of the tall buildings of New York. In my hand I clutched ten fifty-dollar bills – a very handsome surprise, I must admit. I arrived home safely, really none the worse for my absurd adventures, but greatly mystified. Indeed, had it not been for the urgent insistence of my friends I think I should have been disposed to make no complaint to the police of the affair, for I had no wish to incur the enmity of the men who had done this strange deed. And I saw no way of bringing about their arrest. Indeed, I did not know at that time where our journey had led."

Dr. Adair's friends prevailed upon him to lay the matter before the police, however, when he discovered

Edward J. Milliken

Edward J. Milliken

Edward J. Milliken

E E d

E E d d d

Edward J. Milliken

John John

Edward John Milliken

k
k

m m l l l l l

Edward John Milliken

The writing on the crumpled paper – *see p. 102*

in the pocket of his coat a crumpled ball of paper which seemed to yield some clues to the mystery.

"I recall now," the Doctor said, the day after reaching home, "that when I stood at the window with the revolver against my back I nervously clutched a crumpled paper which I found in the pocket of the dressing gown. I distinctly recall feeling the paper when I started my little speech. I assume I must have unconsciously rolled it into a little ball and kept it in my hand, and some time later thrust it in the pocket of my coat. I was so agitated that I may very well have done so. Most certainly it came from the dressing gown, for I am sure I have never seen it before. This gown, you will recall, had been given to me by 'Lester.' It was about his size and my own – rather small."

The paper (see accompanying illustration) was duly examined by Dr. Adair's friends, who mistook it for a private code or cipher. It remained for Detective Anson to point out the true significance of the find and to follow up the case intelligently.

Had you been Detective Anson, what would you have made of the mystery? The questions to be answered are:

1. *Why was Dr. Adair rather than any other person kidnapped by the two men?* (Credit 1.)

2. *Why didn't they make him sign the papers which he expected would be brought upstairs for his signature?* (Credit 2.)

3. *Who was E. J. Milliken?* (Credit 1.)

4. *Which were the two cities through which the Doctor and his captors passed to reach their destination?* (Credit 2.)

5. *In which city did the Doctor probably stay overnight?* (Credit 1.)

6. *What did the captors of Dr. Adair gain by their strange scheme?* (Credit 2.)

7. *Where would you have sought for or E. J. Milliken?* (Credit 1.)

Credit Score:

NO. 15

THE SHOOTING OF "WHISPER" MALLOY

ONE OF THE MOST INTERESTING detective problems that ever confronted the Norville police was found last year in the circumstances of the so-called "highway killings" in the South Chelsea district of Norville. The police were first informed of the tragedy by Ivan Poskoff, a Polish milkman of South Norville. Poskoff, while driving around the curve of the Upper Norville highway at 4 P.M., discovered the roadster on the side of the lonely highway with its strange pair of dead men in the front seat.

Strange companions, indeed, thought the Norville police when they arrived upon the scene, for the body sprawled over the steering, wheel was that of none other than "Whisper" Malloy, invaluable stool pigeon of the Norville authorities for several years. And the body next it was that of "Long Dan" Shutz, a notorious Long Island yeggman and sworn enemy of the stool pigeon. It was "Whisper's" car.

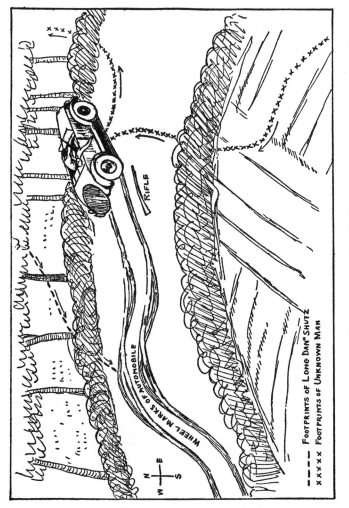

The telltale scene on the Upper Norville Highway, reconstructed according to data furnished by Lieutenant Brown of the Norville Police.

"Whisper" had been shot in the forehead, just above the left eye, with a bullet from an Enfield rifle. The coroner established that he must have been rendered unconscious immediately and that he must have died a very few seconds later. On the road at the right side of the car (see accompanying diagram) lay an Enfield rifle. The bullet found in Malloy's skull at the autopsy was later identified by rifle experts as having been fired from this rifle.

The police were amazed to observe that the tall, pock-marked youth, known as "Long Dan" Shutz, had been shot from the right side, two bullets having entered his neck. A Winchester rifle lay between the two bodies, close beside "Whisper's" sprawled form. The stock of the Winchester rested on the leather-cushioned seat, almost touching the right hip of the stool pigeon; its barrel point rested on the low windshield. The autopsy on the body of Shutz identified the two bullets which had slain him as having come from this Winchester rifle.

Just what had happened? A duel? How came the enemy of the murdered stool pigeon into the car? And which died first? There were no clear fingerprints on either rifle. "Whisper" had on gloves; "Long Dan" had none.

The Norville detectives were able to make out (on the surface of the highway and its neighboring fields) many footprints which aided in a partial solution of the mystery. The auto tracks were also studied.

The detectives knew that both victims were men with more than one enemy, but they had scarcely expected to see them die together under such mystifying circumstances. What do you deduce?

The questions to be answered are:

1. *Who killed "Whisper" Malloy?* (Credit 2.)

2. *Who killed "Long Dan" Shutz?* (Credit 2.)

3. *Which was shot first?* (Credit 1.)

4. *How came "Long Dan" in the stool pigeon's car?* (Credit 3.)

5. *Why did the unknown man go to the car?* (Credit 2.)

Credit score:

A NOTE ON THE TYPE

The Baffle Book has been set in Plantin, a face cut for Monotype in 1913 under the direction of Frank Hinman Pierpont. The fruit of Pierpont's research in the collection of the Plantin-Moretus Museum in Antwerp, Plantin is based on types cut in the sixteenth century by the peripatetic French typographer Robert Granjon. Unlike the more studious revivals released during Stanley Morison's tenure at Monotype, Plantin was freely adapted to the demands of modern printing: its strokes were thickened and its descenders shortened, making it a popular type for printers of periodicals. In fact, Plantin was so successful in this realm that it would later serve as one of the models for Morison's own Times New Roman. A face of considerable heft and warmth, Plantin was particularly popular among European printers and was one of the first types to be adapted for use in offset lithography.

★ ★
★

Design and composition by
Carl W. Scarbrough

ANSWER SECTION

Who Murdered Ellington Breese?

1. Walters, the nephew, murdered Ellington Breese. (Credit 5.)

2. The police deduced that Walters was the murderer from the fact that the flies and the mosquitoes found dead were on the windowsills instead of around the room. This indicated that the gas had permeated the room *after* dawn, for the following reasons: a poison gas, powerful enough to kill a human being, would kill instantly such insects as flies and mosquitoes. Therefore they must have been at the windows when overtaken by the gas. From this it can be deduced that it was light at the time, since such insects, in a dark room, are attracted to the windows by the light coming in beneath partially drawn shades. It may be logically considered to be very improbable that so many insects would have been found on the window sills had the instantaneously fatal gas been released in the darkness of the night. (Credit 5.)

Observation of this clue led the detectives to another terrific grilling of Walters, who eventually broke down and confessed to the crime. He had stolen down at the break of dawn. Desperate losses in wildcat speculation, it later developed, had driven Walters to the deed. He was subsequently convicted and executed early in 1926.

No. 2
THE EVIDENCE IN THE JAPANNED BOX

1. A guest stole the Elgin emerald from the japanned box which the owner, Stephen Lerian, had left carelessly upon the living-room table. (Credit 5.)

2. The thief was Miss Charlotte Grainger, as indicated by the telltale thumb mark on the rim of the inside of the cover of the japanned box. (Credit 5.)

Charlotte Grainger's thumbprint was the only one which was identical in its ridge markings with the thumbprint on the japanned box cover.

The distinctive feature of both prints is the arch formation of the ridges.

The ridges are classified according to types – loops, whorls, arches. For instance Colonel Blue's thumbprint would be classified as distinguished by its whorls; that of Mr. Hay by its loops; and Charlotte Grainger's was the only one distinguished by its arches.

The dangerous aftermath of Stephen Lerian's private investigation into the disappearance of his emerald was no fault of his. The unfortunate girl, whose kleptomaniacal impulses were unknown even to her uncle and aunt, Mr. and Mrs. Archibald Hay, was herself the cause of the unpleasant publicity which the whole case received. Lerian refrained from broaching his shocking discovery to the girl's uncle until she and

the Hays had returned to the Hay home. Her uncle decided to search her room. The niece, coming upon her uncle just as he had located the missing jewel in her dresser, flew at him in a desperate assault and seriously injured him with a paper cutter which she had snatched up. Every effort was made to hush up the affair, but it was revealed to the police through servants who had suffered from the girl's ungovernable bursts of temper. It was this that forced the Hays to agree to her confinement in a private sanitarium. The Hays, it must be recorded, placed no blame whatever upon Lerian for his methods in detecting the theft.

No. 3
THE ELEVATED TRAIN MYSTERY
PART I

1. The body fell to the sidewalk under Cho Sing's windows from the *roof of the last car* of the elevated railroad train which swung around the curve about 2:28 A.M. (Credit 4.)

Captain Danforth deduced as follows:

The body was not on the tracks, according to the track walker's testimony, just before the train came to the spot. It had not come from the platforms or windows of the cars of the train, according to all available testimony of passengers and guards. Upon striking the sidewalk the body had enough impetus or spin in it to

roll under an awning attached to the building in which Cho Sing's restaurant was housed. Therefore it was highly probable that the snap of the end car of the train making the curve was the cause of the impetus – an impetus *away* from the path of the train and *toward* the building. While it was *possible* that the body might have been flung from a window above Cho Sing's, or from the roof, onto the car's roof, it was extremely improbable that the murderer would have done so, because Cho Sing's restaurant was open and crowded. To have done so would have invited detection. Therefore, Captain Danforth reasoned, it was almost certain that the murder had occurred uptown somewhere, and that the murderer had thrown the body on the roof of the car to get it carried far from the scene of the crime.

2. The roof of the rear end of the train is what should have been searched particularly for clues which might lead to the apprehension of the murderer. (Credit 1.)

How Captain Danforth did search there and what he found and deduced therefrom, you will see in Part II of "The Elevated Transit Mystery" which begins on page 29.

PART II

Captain Danforth directed search immediately to the "zone of suspicion" which lay between One Hundred

and Eleventh Street and the Ninety-ninth Street stations of the Elevated Transit Company's Tenth Avenue line. (Credit 2.)

Captain Danforth reasoned thus: He eliminated as *improbable* the "zone of suspicion" nearest the One Hundred and Fifty-first Street station, in view of the testimony of Inspector Monahan. (Monahan had said the body was not on the roof of Train No. 34 when he watched it pass downtown from the bridge at the One Hundred and Twentieth Street station.)

Captain Danforth then eliminated as *impossible* the "zone of suspicion" which centered at the Seventy-fourth Street station. He did this because the Weather Bureau report showed that the shower had burst on the uptown region at 2:20 A.M., at which time Train No. 34 had only reached the Ninetieth Street station on its downtown journey. The roof of the train must have been thoroughly wetted by the time it reached the "zone of suspicion" at Seventy-fourth Street, and if the body had been thrown on in that zone there could not have been a perfectly dry spot apparent on the otherwise soaked roof of the car. But such a dry spot, in the shape of a sprawled body, *had* been found on the roof of the rear-end car. Therefore, Captain Danforth deduced, the body must have been thrown on *before* the shower began. Hence his selection of the "zone of suspicion" which lay between the One Hun-

dred and Eleventh and the Ninety-ninth Street stations, for the train had passed through it *before* the shower had begun.

How the detectives searched in the suspected zone, what they found there, and how Captain Danforth finally located the murder scene and captured the murderer, you will learn in Part III of "The Elevated Transit Mystery" which begins on page 33.

PART III

1. The building in which the detective found the final clues was that in which the Palace Gardens, a dance hall, was located. (Credit 2.)

2. Captain Danforth deduced that the dance-hall building, rather than any other, was the place of greatest suspicion, thus: the soles of the shoes of the victim had been found dry, not wet; the water which had soaked other parts of his clothing *on the back*, had been warded off the slippery, waxed soles of his shoes, as observed by the police when they first examined him. Almost certainly, then, the man had been dancing just previous to his death, and this pointed to the Palace Gardens. (Credit 1.)

Captain Danforth, after tracing back the body from Cho Sing's at Forty-eighth Street to the Palace Gardens dance-hall region at One Hundred and Sixth Street, began a painstaking examination of all persons

known to have been at the dance hall that night. While no clues within the dance hall could be found, either on the roof or on window sills, the proprietors of the hall admitted that the evening had been disturbed by sounds as if of a brawl in the men's washroom a little after 2 A.M. It had quieted down quickly, and the proprietors had thought nothing of it, for such sounds were not uncommon at the Gardens.

Captain Danforth put a young woman detective on the case. She visited the Palace Gardens frequently, posing as the jazziest of flappers, and within a week had learned two important facts. First, several of the girls who had frequented the place and might therefore have been in a position to testify as to events of the night had left town suddenly on Sunday. Second, there had been a Porto Rican chauffeur here that night – dark, handsome, and in a dress suit. No one could be found who had seen him go home.

Meanwhile the victim had been identified by the press as José Racheta, Porto Rican chauffeur and race-track devotee, temporarily out of work. Captain Danforth discovered that Racheta had entered the Palace Gardens alone, in the possession of $550 won that afternoon on a horse race. By tracing the girl habitués of the Palace Gardens to Boston, where they had been sent to get them out of the way, Captain Danforth was able to learn the names of two men seen to have

entered the washroom after Racheta did so a little after 2 A.M. on that Sunday.

Both men were arrested in a car on Brooklyn Bridge eleven days after the finding of Racheta's body. In the pockets of Alexander Kargos, the elder, were found cuff links identified later as Racheta's. Petrino Guido, an Italian window cleaner, living in the Bronx, was the other suspect. Both broke under the third degree and confessed to the robbery and murder of Racheta in the dance-hall washroom.

Quickly cutting out all identification marks from the clothes, Guido, the window cleaner, had clung to the window sill with his knees while he had leaned out and dropped the body on the "L" train as it sped by, scarcely two feet below and three feet away.

Captain Danforth was promoted and the murderers were electrocuted.

No. 4
THE PROBLEM OF THE BANDIT'S TORN NOTE

1. The lobby of the Hotel La Salle was the place named in the note for a meeting of "Red" Sam Gunther's band. (Credit 5.)

2. Date of meeting – Wednesday noon. (Credit 5.)

The Chicago police deduced this information from the fragments of the torn note, which they reconstructed as follows:

Meet us La Salle
lobby prompt at
noon Wednesday

Plain-clothes policemen acquainted with the facts of Gunther's adherents were present in force and bagged four men long wanted by the authorities.

No. 5
THE SANDY PENINSULA FOOTPRINT MYSTERY

1. At the spot marked 2 on the diagram Mrs. Strang and her escort (woman and man) were strolling along the beach side by side when they were overtaken by Revington Strang on horseback. Strang evidently leaned down from his saddle, seized his wife, and lifted her up onto the horse. Her escort (man) was forced to step aside to avoid being run down, as Strang's horse passed in front of him. (Credit 1.)

2. Man *ran* after the horse, then swerved up the beach toward the pile of rocks at 3 on the diagram, with the evident intention of hiding to observe the movements of the horseman. Then, noticing that the rider had almost reached the end of the beach, he waited to see what he would do. (Credit 1.)

3. At 3, noticing that the horseman had turned north toward the road, man turned and made a short cut to the road, knowing that the horseman would

have to ride past him to leave the peninsula. (Credit 1.)

4. Near 4 man undoubtedly waited in the bushes for the horse to come, then leaped out, stopped the horse, and dragged the horseman to the ground. (No footprints showed on the macadamized road.) Presumably they fought in the road, as there were no footprints or other marks showing the struggle. Man presumably knocked Strang out by a terrific blow on the chin. Discovering that he had killed his adversary, man dragged the body underneath the bushes at the side of the road. Footprints around the body show that he dragged it by the feet, stood a moment looking at it, and then stepped to the side of the woman, Mrs. Strang, who was also standing looking at the body. (Credit 1.)

5. From 4 to 5 on the diagram there are no footprints of woman, but man's footprints, wide apart and pointing straight ahead instead of toeing out (compare man's footprints 1 to 2 with his footprints 4 to 5) indicate that he carried a heavy weight from 4 to 5. From 5 to 6 the footprints had undoubtedly been covered by the *incoming* tide, but the presence of the woman's footprints from 6 to 7 show that she must have been with man. Therefore it is possible to deduce that she might have fainted at 4, while looking at the body of her husband. She was being *carried* by man between 4 and 5. (Credit 1.)

6. Man carried woman down to the water, where presumably he revived her, near 5, by splashing water on her face. (Credit 1.)

7. Between 5 and 6 they walked along the sand near the margin of the sea, but their footprints had been covered by the incoming tide before the detectives arrived on the scene. (Credit 1.)

8. Between 6 and 7, where footprints of man and woman are again visible, they walked side by side, the closeness of the footprints showing that Mrs. Strang, still weak, was being supported by her escort. (Credit 1.)

9. At 7 their footprints are again covered by the tide, but it is obvious that they returned to their starting point (somewhere seaward between 1 and 7), where they must have left their canoe, launched it and left the peninsula. The marks left by the canoe (necessarily pulled up on the sand) had been covered by the tide when the detectives arrived; but the testimony of the lighthouse keeper showed that a man and a woman had arrived by canoe. In all probability they left the peninsula in this way. (Credit 1.)

10. It can be deduced that the horse, after the event at 4 on the diagram, probably ran off down the road, for it left no footprints on the beach after once turning into the road. (Actually, the horse was found later in the fields near Parkville, several miles south of San Serena.) (Credit 1.)

The murderer of Revington Strang, undoubtedly Mrs. Strang's escort of that afternoon, was later identified by the detectives as Rupert Hardesty, a former welterweight champion of Yale University. Hardesty and Mrs. Strang never returned to San Serena, fleeing that afternoon, it later developed, to San Francisco, where they took passage on false passports on the ill-fated *Emerald Queen*, bound for Yokohama. The *Emerald Queen*, it will be recalled, went down with all on board during the great typhoon of 1922, off the Japanese coast.

No. 6

The Case of the Stolen Van Dyck

1. Harry Sims, day attendant at the Farjeon Museum, wrote the ransom note about the stolen Van Dyck. (Credit 10.)

The detective cleverly identified the handwriting of Sims (as given in the application for a position) with the disguised handwriting of the ransom note. Sims was arrested on suspicion; and later developments in the case brought about a confession.

Superficially it might even seem that the handwriting in the ransom note most nearly resembled that of Gregg, the night watchman, but on closer examination it will be seen that, good disguise as it is, several characteristic details were overlooked by Sims, most notably the crossing of the t's. The crossings on his t's

14

were not horizontal but tended toward an arch in style – an unusual and distinctive evidence.

Sims's handwriting, moreover, is obviously that of a person with considerable dexterity with a pen. And the writing in the ransom note, with its stiff and carefully made strokes, indicates that great pains had been taken to have it appear different from the natural hand of the writer. Neither Weaver nor Gregg show in their hand-writing the excellent control of the pen that Sims has.

In attempting to disguise his handwriting, Sims forgot another point: he failed to eliminate from the ransom note his habit of breaking off the stroke in the midst of a word and then beginning with a new stroke. (See the space between the "pain" and "ting" in "paint-ing," and between the "s" and the "t" in "strickly," etc.

The *dénouement* of the Sims case is noteworthy in that it involved what was probably the first criminal catch effected jointly by aëroplane and radio. The museum trustees had taken precautions to have a radio sending apparatus installed in the rear car of the train; and aëroplanes acting as patrols in the distant wake of the train. The thief and his confederates, they believed, had obviously imitated the Charlie Ross kidnappers in their method of instructing for payment of the ran-som. But the kidnappers of the famous portrait had for-gotten how times had changed since the 1870s, when there was no way of broadcasting from a moving train.

Eighty miles out of Somerset, in the midst of a four-mile level spot, a man with two yellow flags rose from behind a pile of ties and waved to the end of the train. The bag was thrown over promptly, and the museum representative, to lessen suspicion, turned in a leisurely way and walked slowly back into the car. The train did not slacken speed, but within ten seconds the alarm was being broadcast to listening radio stations all along the route. The man with the yellow flags had picked up the bag, opened and examined its contents with satisfaction, and hurried down an adjacent lane, where an automobile stood ready.

The police of the towns in the region were prepared for quick response. Within ten minutes six searching parties had begun the hunt, and all roads for a radius of twenty miles were being watched. Even so, it is probable that the fugitive would have escaped had it not been for the aëroplane then following the train at a distance of three miles. Scouts with field telescopes in the plane were attracted to the general scene of the getaway and later spied a car travelling at tremendous speed toward the foothills of the Adirondacks on a rough country road. By flying faster and in a more direct line, the aviators were able to outstrip the car and drop messages in neighboring towns. The aviators lost the automobile in the Franchette Woods, but by

landing quickly they were able to telephone directions to the local police which resulted in the capture of Sims's confederates with the money intact.

Sims confessed after brief questioning that he had cut the Van Dyck from its frame and smuggled it out of the museum in the arm of his raincoat on the evening of May 3rd, when the night watchman was late. His confederates included his second cousin and a former clerk in a Somerset art shop. The portrait was recovered in perfect condition from a safety deposit box in a Utica bank, where the clerk had put it the day following the theft.

Sims and his confederates were convicted and received heavy terms.

No. 7
THE DUNDURY WAYSIDE MYSTERY

1. The murder car had Vacuum Cup Balloon Tires, as was shown by the distinctive pattern of the tracks. (Credit 2.)

2. It could be deduced that there were at least two men in the car. The body of the girl had evidently been thrown out while the car was *in motion*. Doing this would almost certainly have required a driver plus the man who hurled the body. (Credit 2.)

3. The body had been there only a short time, for

the dress and stockings were *splashed* with dew in several places. If it had lain there most of the night the clothing would have been soaked with dew all over, not splashed. (Credit 2.)

4. The car was traveling from east to west. The forward momentum of the body in the direction in which the car was traveling when the body was thrown out caused the bushes and twigs to be flattened out in that direction. (*See illustration.*) Also, the body was lying with the head toward the west. The fact that the skirt was comparatively smooth down over the legs also showed the forward momentum of the body toward the west. If it had been thrown out with its feet in the direction in which the car was traveling the skirt would have been blown up instead of down. (Credit 2.)

5. The missing slipper was not found near the body. Therefore, Constable Barge reasoned that it might have fallen off in the car at the time of the throwing of the body. If this had happened the slipper probably would have been thrown out later. A search along the road might locate the black patent leather slipper. Telltale finger marks of the murderer might logically be expected to have remained on its highly polished surface. (Credit 1.)

6. In the bushes along the road to the *west* of the place where the body was found would be the logical place to look first for the missing slipper, for the per-

son throwing the body out of the car would probably wish to get rid of such damning evidence as quickly as its presence was discovered. (Credit 1.)

Soon after the Middletown police were notified by Constable Barge, the family of Ada Carrista, a Buffalo stenographer, broadcast the news of the abduction of their youngest daughter from her home. The Carristas were of Mexican extraction and were probably being systematically blackmailed up to a short time before the tragedy. It was believed that the blackmailers had intended to hold the girl for ransom and return her after additional sums had been paid.

A car with the Vacuum Cup Balloon tires was found abandoned in an alley in Middletown that afternoon. Later a man lurking in the vicinity was arrested on suspicion by plain-clothesmen of the Middletown police force. He proved to be a member of the abduction gang of four, and through papers found in his pocket the others were found in Middletown. The leader of the gang, Miguel Rodon, committed suicide as the detectives knocked at his hotel door.

Rodon's fingerprints were taken and compared with the fingerprints on the black slipper which Constable Barge found in the bushes a half mile west of the scene of the Dunbury tragedy. They matched.

The others of the gang are still in jail.

No. 8
THE TOLEDO DEATH THREAT CLUE

A mutilated copy of the *Saturday Evening Post*, which was found in McHarg's room, proved McHarg guilty of sending the clipped-word death threat letter. (Credit 10.)

The word "Saturday" in the pasted note was in the distinctive style of type used in the words "*Saturday Evening Post*" which are printed at the top of each page of that publication. Observation of this fact had led the detectives to expect that a mutilated copy of this magazine might be found in the room. The clipping fitted to the mutilated page.

McHarg confessed, with more braggadocio than discretion, and was later sentenced to the reformatory for two years.

No. 9
THE SCULPTOR'S STUDIO MYSTERY

1. Reginald Lamont, the sculptor, was murdered by his wife. (Credit 2.)

2. Detective Coldstream deduced that the wife must have been in the studio on the afternoon of the murder. From the parts of the words "ack" and "Mes," on the fragment of paper found in the fireplace and

from the mesh design around the words, he believed that it was part of an envelope used as a container for a hair net. He found on investigation that it was, in fact, a part of the upper right-hand corner of a "Venida" hair-net envelope.

Hair nets are made in various colors and shades: Auburn, Blonde, Dark Brown, Black, etc. the "ack" could be only part of the word Black. Lamont's wife was a black-haired Spaniard; the other suspect, a blonde. It seemed highly probable, therefore, that the wife had lied when she testified that she had not been in the studio on the day of the murder. (Credit 5.)

3. The motive of the murderess was probably not only jealousy, but also revenge for an insult. (Credit 1.)

4. The head of the statue had been smashed, but no other part of the body. The wife, a woman of thirty-seven, had posed for the statue. The younger woman had recently posed for Lamont for a study of her head. Detective Coldstream deduced that the sculptor, using as a model the study of the head he had made of Miss Halverson, had changed the face of the statue some-time after the wife had finished posing, and that Mrs. Lamont, coming unexpectedly to the studio, had been infuriated by the discovery (especially since she had probably heard of her husband's relations with Helga Halverson). (Credit 2.)

Then, the detective reasoned, the wife had snatched up the mallet in her anger and had struck the head of the statue. Lamont interfered to protect his work and was attacked by his wife in a frenzy.

Mrs. Lamont pleaded temporary insanity. She admitted at the trial that she had come unexpectedly to her husband's studio on that afternoon. It was a windy day, and immediately upon entering she went to the mirror above the mantel to smooth her hair. She then recalled that she had in her bag a hair net, and put it on, having discarded the envelope in the fire at her feet. As she was finishing she caught sight in the mirror of the changed face of the statue, and, in her own words at the trial, "remembered nothing more until after the terrible thing had happened."

The jury however, did not believe it, and she is now in prison.

No. 10
The Beals–Bligh Anonymous Letters

1. Lady Beals-Bligh, Sir Chatham's wife, sent the anonymous letters. (Credit 2.)

2. This can be deduced from:

(a) The American, rather than the English manner of spelling "dishonorable" in the first letter. It was not spelled with a "u."

(b) Somewhat similar misspellings in the first anonymous letter and Lady Beals-Bligh's forgiveness letter to her husband: "incontrovertable" instead of the correct "incontrovertible"; and, in the forgiveness letter, "seperate" instead of the correct "separate."

(c) Similarity in style of construction of sentences in the first anonymous letter and the wife's forgiveness letter: long sentences with many hanging clauses. (Credit 5.)

3. Suzette, the French maid, was almost certainly the accomplice in the case. She probably mailed the first letter in London and wrote the second from dictation over the telephone and mailed it in Hilton the suburb. (Credit 3.)

The private detective, former Inspector Givott of Scotland Yard, reasoned it out for his colleagues some years later as follows:

"Lady Beals-Bligh undoubtedly had heard the common gossip of Sir Chatham's renewed carrying on with the Austrian baroness. She loved her husband and wanted to end the affair without destroying his respect for her. *Open* charges against him, she believed, would mean the end of their marriage, so she hit upon the plan of frightening him by an anonymous letter.

"There can be no doubt that she prepared the first

letter in Tirringham and sent Suzette to London with it for posting. This, Suzette must have done immediately upon her arrival in London on the morning of the day before Lady Beals-Bligh's town visit. She mailed it at the Paddington Station.

"After Suzette had gone, it must have occurred to Lady Beals-Bligh that the first letter was much more ominous in its sound than she had intended. She feared that her husband might turn it over to the police or do something desperate, fearing a *public* exposure. Therefore, she must have communicated with Suzette, who, I infer, was probably staying overnight at the well-known French tavern in Hilton, the suburb. It would have been natural for her to do so, since her mistress was coming to town the following day. (Undoubtedly they had made plans to meet in town.)

"The second anonymous letter was postmarked from Hilton and was in a slightly different hand printing. I believe therefore that Lady Beals-Bligh told Suzette to write a second letter and mail it immediately. This read: 'What I mean is, I will tell your wife if it does not stop.' That would limit Sir Chatham's fears and would indicate that no public exposure was intended.

"Lady Beals-Bligh and Suzette met in London the next morning and proceeded together to the town house, as if they had just arrived from Tirringham

together. The wife must have been stunned when her husband confessed his infidelity. Her plan had worked so beautifully for her that she was compelled to pretend that she would not forgive him. Or possibly she had hoped that the gossip was not true after all, and was really disappointed. At any rate, she probably intended even then to forgive him. She went back to their Tirringham place and did not let much time go by before writing him a letter from there, offering peace.

"As for Hobbs, I doubt that he knew anything of the matter. His presence in Hilton must have been a coincidence, else he had never volunteered the information that he had been there. As a matter of fact I later learned that Hobbs had met the innkeeper through friends of Suzette some months before. No doubt Suzette told the innkeeper to say nothing to anyone of her being at the inn, since she was supposed to be still at Tirringham. Of course Hobbs guessed that Suzette had something to do with it the moment he saw the Hilton postmark, but could hardly afford to voice suspicion of his fiancée to Sir Chatham.

"Naturally, when I saw how matters lay, I recommended to Sir Chatham's counsellor that we report a dead wall and advise dropping the matter. And I am told that they are still married."

No. 11
Messer Bellini's Report to the Doge

1. Torcello was able to poison Geronimo alone, and not others, by a slight move of the thumb when pouring him a cup of wine from the pitcher. The vessel was designed for such a deed. Between the tiny hole in the flower blossom and the tiny hole under the lip of the pitcher ran a very narrow channel or tube *inside the clay of the pitcher.* This tube had been filled with poison. According to a law of physics, when Torcello kept his thumb firmly over the hole in the blossom, and poured, *wine only* went into the cup. But when he took his thumb off, poison began to trickle out. It issued from the hole under the lip of the pitcher and merged inconspicuously with the wine stream.

Since the movement of control was almost imperceptible to even a suspicious observer, the Cavalier's villainy was not easily detected. The accident of Baptista's blowing under the lip of the pitcher revealed the existence of a hole there and a hole in the blossom where the bubble appeared. She had blown back some remaining drops of the poison. (Credit 5.)

2. If Baptista had helped herself to wine from the pitcher she would probably have been poisoned. Presumably her hands were much smaller than Torcello's, and it is not likely that she would, entirely by accident,

press her thumb against the flower with the little hole. (Credit 2.)

3. As far as the person making the report (Messer Bellini) was able to deduce, the pitcher was made with an open fretwork around the neck, except the part near the lip of the pitcher (*see illustration*), in order to make the working of the device more certain. If the wine were poured out fast, there might not be time for a sufficient dose of poison to mingle with the stream of wine. Obviously, the fretwork was a cunning contrivance designed to force the pourer to pour slowly, or to make slow pouring appear natural. If the wine were poured swiftly, it would naturally come in such a wide stream that it would spill through the openwork. The openwork therefore somewhat aided the murderer in masking his infernal design. (Credit 3.)

Messer Bellini's report to the Doge closes with an elaborate description of the pitcher and urges the arrest and imprisonment of the Cavaliere Torcello. It is interesting to note that Doge Arbasini agreed, casting the murderer into the famous dungeon of the Doge's Palace and later having him dragged head downward through the streets at the tail of a horse – a favorite Venetian method of execution.

The origin of the poison pitcher could probably be traced far into antiquity, although this is, so far as is

known, the first record of the amazingly ingenious device. Later these pitchers became quite popular in Venice.

No. 12

The Mystery of the Murdered Physician

1. The murderer of Dr. Winthrop Brett was a woman. (Credit 1.)

2. This was proved by the single sheet of newspaper found lying in front of the radiator. Inspector Marquard deduced that the long, narrow shriveled mark on the page must have been made by the drying of a damp stocking. He reasoned that the murderess reached over the body to get the little green books from the wall safe; that in so doing her stocking came in contact with the large bloodstain on the breast of the doctor's coat. He knew that in 1926 skirts were worn very short and that stockings were usually light in color. (Credit 9.)

"Unable in any way to *hide* the damning stain on her stocking," Marquard writes, "and knowing that the valet would not return until six, she removed her stocking, washed out the stain, and went to put the stocking along the top of the radiator where it would dry quickly. Seeing the newspaper near by, she tore off a page, laid it on top of the radiator, and laid her

stocking along it so that the stocking would dry without any dirt or rust from the radiator – a very natural action. She would probably have had to wash almost the whole leg of the stocking, for silk stockings show very plainly any marks left by water.

"After the stocking had dried and she had removed it from the radiator, the piece of newspaper was wafted off the radiator by the hot air rising from it; or possibly she carelessly knocked it off when removing the stocking.

"The fact that she had left the cold water running also pointed to her having washed away a bloodstain, for cold water is much preferable to hot water for removing bloodstains.

"It may be argued that a woman, under these circumstances, would scarcely have dared to run the risk of lingering in the apartment long enough to wash her stocking; but to appear on the street without having done so would be far more dangerous. She had no way whatever of hiding the conspicuous stain. To wash and dry the stocking sufficiently to permit wearing it would take less than twenty minutes. Moreover, very soon after she had killed the physician she must have realized that her shots had not been heard, for no one came running. She probably had been intimate with Brett and probably knew that there would be no other appointments that afternoon but her own. For I cannot

doubt that she was the person who telephoned at I P.M. and then overheard the doctor release Wilkins till six.

"It is also obvious that the murderess was in a mood for playing a desperate hand, for when she failed to force the physician (perhaps at the pistol point) to *give* her the books, she shot him and took them.

"As to her identity, of course I know nothing; but it seems probable that she had been one of the doctor's patients, that she had at some time made indiscreet confessions to him, of a personal nature, which he had recorded and possibly used to obtain a hold on her. And that she finally rebelled is certain.

"I should imagine that the 'little green books' have been long since destroyed and that the lady's identity will never become known."

No. 13
The Affair of the French Spy

I. Mlle G., the French spy, communicated the message to her confederate in the dot and dash of international Morse Code hastily embroidered as clocks on ordinary plain silk stockings. (Credit 7.)

2. The message read:

Left leg	· · · ·	— · · ·
	H	B
Right leg	· · — — —	— · · · ·
	2	6

HB26 was the secret-service number of the treacherous spy that the French were seeking. (Credit 3.)

Although it is not recorded whether or not Mlle G. knew that her confederate could read the code, this would seem unnecessary, since she might at least be certain that he would observe and copy the design and have it decoded later.

No. 14
The Kidnapping of Dr. Adair

1. Dr. Adair was singled out for kidnapping because he happened to bear a strong facial resemblance to the man whose impersonation was essential to the plans of the kidnappers. (Credit 1.)

2. The kidnappers did not require him to sign the papers for two reasons: the signature had to be a good forgery of the signature of E. J. Milliken, and Dr. Adair's handwriting would not have answered the purpose; secondly, because a passing glance at the papers would have given Adair a clue to the transaction and put the police on the trail of the kidnappers. (Credit 2.)

3. E. J. Milliken was the man impersonated innocently by Dr. Adair under duress. (Credit 1.)

4. Dr. Adair and his kidnappers passed through Philadelphia (the first large city referred to). This was obvious from the distance from New York and the

shouts of the newsboys selling the Philadelphia *Evening Bulletin.* The second city passed through was Baltimore, which can be deduced from the time elapsed and the newsboys' shouts while selling the Baltimore *Evening Sun.* No other large cities, which can be reached by motor in the time specified, have evening newspapers of those names. (Credit 2.)

5. Washington, D.C., was the city in which the party stayed overnight. This can be deduced with approximate certainty from the distance from Baltimore, from the marked decrease in the noise of the street traffic, and from the smoothness of the pavements and frequent curves. The many circles of the asphalt avenues and streets of Washington constitute a distinctive characteristic of the city. (Credit 1.)

6. The captors of Dr. Adair undoubtedly gained possession of a large sum of money by their engineering of the fraud obviously committed. It is clear from the circumstances that considerable must have been at stake to justify the risk of kidnapping an adult and conveying him so far. And it is also clear that the kidnappers were successful in their transaction, for they compensated Dr. Adair when they need not have done so. (Credit 2.)

7. E. J. Milliken should have been sought on some one of the few lonely islands of the world where ships touch only occasionally. (Credit 1.)

Detective Anson deduced from the reported conversation of the kidnappers that the man who was to be the victim of the fraud (E. J. Milliken) was far away and unlikely to return.

Detective Anson has written of the case as follows:

"There are some points which will never be cleared up unless Baldassare is caught, and I am of the opinion that he never will be. But the main points of the conspiracy can now be stated.

"The tall, florid-faced man who first startled Dr. Adair by his cry 'Good God! *Milliken!*' (in the hotel lobby) was obviously not addressing his companion, as the Doctor thought, but calling his companion's attention to Dr. Adair, who, he thought, *was Milliken.*

"The tall, florid-faced man, as we later established, was Rory O'Connor, small-town confidence man and card sharp – a slow-witted fellow compared with his smaller companion, who engineered the scheme. This was Baldassare, the Italian-American who has been wanted for some years on much bigger stuff.

"I have no doubt that Baldassare, with his quicker wit, immediately saw that it was not Milliken but a man closely resembling him, and it must have flashed across his mind that Milliken's 'double' (Dr. Adair) should be followed but not met face to face. Therefore he hurried O'Connor away to escape encountering Dr. Adair.

"Upon taking up the investigation I had no idea, of

course, who Milliken could be. I only knew from the crumpled paper which Adair brought from 'Lester's' dressing gown that *someone* had been practising the imitation of the signature of E. J. Milliken and therefore that Milliken and 'Lester' were probably not the same man. Milliken, then, could be only the man mysteriously referred to by 'Lester' in the phrase: 'Nobody around here has seen him in twenty years.'

"Impersonation of a man who has been away a long time led me to suspect that the man had suddenly acquired or inherited valuable property and knew nothing of it. And that the daring kidnappers were taking advantage of their bull-headed luck in encountering Dr. Adair, by making him pose at some transaction whereby money was forthcoming to Milliken and pocketing it themselves. Once given a reasonably good 'double,' clever forgery would turn the trick for the conspirators. And we may be sure that the men putting up the money, whoever they were, were getting a good bargain in return. For they too were obviously pleased that 'E. J. Milliken' had come to Washington and was ready to close the deal. It was clear from the happenings in the house at Washington that the preparations for the actual signing of the deal had been going on for some time through 'Lester' posing as 'Mr. Devore,' attorney for Milliken. The fact that the other parties to the deal had apparently insisted

on getting a look at the long-vanished Milliken indicated that the transaction was big enough to warrant taking some precaution.

"As it turned out, I was quite wrong in thinking that Milliken had inherited money. The conspiracy involved a lease of oil land in Texas on property he had bought as a young man. It was a simple matter to infer Dr. Adair's trip to Washington. There I sought in vain for the recording of a deed of property from E. J. Milliken. There was no trace. But a friend of mine in the oil business, to whom I had told something of the case, noted a squib in an oil trade journal a week later which gave me all the clues needed. It set forth that the El Dorado Oil Improvement Company had just leased a large tract in the western part of Texas from E. J. Milliken of Fredericksburg, Va., at the highest rental paid for similar land in many years!

"Identifying the conspirators through the El Dorado Company was easy, but we never actually caught up with them. The initial payment on the lease – $82,000 – was never recovered. It had been passed in a certified check to 'E. J. Milliken' by the representatives of the El Dorado Company when 'Lester,' alias Baldassare, posed as Devore, 'Milliken's attorney.' Baldassare of course cashed it soon afterward, having forged Milliken's name to it, just as previously he had forged Milliken's name to the oil land lease agreement.

"As to just where and under what circumstances the real Milliken and the two conspirators had known each other, I have never definitely ascertained. In Fredericksburg I learned that Milliken had left there twenty years before, broken-hearted at the death of his mother, who was his last remaining relative. Some say he went to sea; others that he was known to have gone to England. He left suddenly, selling everything he had to raise money. His Texas property was worthless at that time, or at least he could not sell it.

"But we can be sure that he fell in with the two confidence men (not knowing they were such) when all three were thrown together on some isolated island, where no doubt he stayed while the others eventually returned to America. I have since learned that Baldassare, in his younger days, had been a sea rover and had visited Easter Island, Tristan da Cunha, and other desolate spots. No doubt Milliken had at some time remarked to them that he had property in Texas which was worthless, and Baldassare, upon returning to America, saw in the Texas oil boom a splendid opportunity to put over a neat deal. I do not doubt that he was considering trying to effect the fraudulent sale when luck brought him face to face with Dr. Adair and made it comparatively easy. As a matter of fact, the El Dorado Company had been

seeking Milliken for more than a year but had no idea where to find him. And Milliken, of course, was cut off from newspapers and never knew his luck.

"Inquiries made through the Canadian missionaries who are in touch with the inhabitants of Tristan da Cunha every year or two indicate that an elderly man who died there several years ago may have been Milliken. I have yet to receive confirmation.

"Rory O'Connor is known to have been killed soon after the kidnapping in a drunken brawl in Louisville. But Baldassare is still wanted. There can be no doubt that it was Baldassare. The description of the smaller man in the hotel lobby and the description I received of 'Mr. Devore' from the El Dorado representatives leaves no doubt as to his identity. Only Baldassare of all the known confidence men would have arranged such an elaborate deal. It was characteristically clever of him to overcome Dr. Adair's lack of height by having him stand on a box when addressing the oil men, for Milliken, I find, was a tall man.

"I have been asked why Baldassare went to such pains to produce an impersonator since none of the three oil men seemed to recognize 'Milliken,' or give evidence of knowing him when they 'saw him.' The answer is: Baldassare feared that they might bring to the conference some person from Fredericksburg who

had known Milliken as a young man. Not to have brought 'Milliken' to close the deal might have aroused suspicion. By keeping 'Milliken' on the second floor, pretending that he was ill and could not come down, the conspirators avoided searching scrutiny which close observation would have afforded. As a matter of fact, the oil men were anxious to close the deal and get to drilling their wells, and they had no idea of the elaborate fraud imposed. They had looked up E. J. Milliken's signature of twenty years ago in Fredericksburg and were completely taken in by Baldassare's excellent imitation of it, or rather by his masterly conception of what it would have been twenty years later. For Baldassare, clever forger that he was, was careful not to have it the same as the signature of Milliken as a young man.

"As for Dr. Adair, he never at any time grasped the significance of what was going on about him."

No. 15
The Shooting of "Whisper" Malloy

1. "Long Dan" Shutz killed "Whisper" Malloy. He shot with the Enfield rifle from ambush on the north side of the road. (Credit 2.)

2. The unknown man killed "Long Dan" Shutz. He shot with the Winchester rifle from ambush on the south side of the road after Shutz climbed into the car. (Credit 2.)

3. "Whisper" Malloy must have been shot first. (Credit 1.)

4. The body of "Long Dan" was found in "Whisper" Malloy's car because, after killing Malloy, he rushed from his ambush and jumped into the car to prevent it from running wild, which it had started to do (see automobile tracks). Probably he had righted the wheel and was starting to turn the bend in the road when he was struck by the unknown man's bullets. (Credit 3.)

5. The unknown man went to the car to plant his Winchester near "Whisper," in order to give the impression that the two men had fought a duel. He removed his fingerprints from the Winchester. (Credit 2.)

Though the unknown man was never caught, the Norville detectives were confident that it was but one more incident in the infamous gang war which so disturbed the community the year before. They explained matters as follows:

It was well known in the underworld, they believed, that Shutz was out to get "Whisper." The unknown must have been a member of the Bacardi Rum gang, which was at war with a gang led by Shutz's brother. The unknown probably heard of Shutz's plan to lie in wait for the stool pigeon, and followed him. From the south side of the road he watched the unsuspecting Shutz waiting opposite for the approaching car of

the stool pigeon. The unknown then shot Shutz as described and planted the evidence.

He could then walk away from the scene unarmed, leaving the stage set as if a desperate duel had occurred.